JULIA'S SHILLING

By

Coreen Turner

Copyright © Coreen Turner 2018

This book is sold subject to the condition that it shall not, by way of trade or otherwise, be lent, resold, hired out, or otherwise circulated without the publisher's prior consent in any form of binding or cover other than that in which it is published and without a similar condition including this condition being imposed on the subsequent publisher.

The moral right of Coreen Turner has been asserted.

ISBN-13: 9781726623926

Dedicated to Helen Dunmore 1952-2017
novelist and poet, who realised in her final novel,
'Birdcage Walk', that only a very few people leave
traces in history, and that women's lives particularly
remain largely unrecorded, although through their
existences they change the lives around them and
form the lives of their descendants.

CONTENTS

INTRODUCTION 1
CHAPTER 1. *Uninvited Guests* 2
CHAPTER 2. *A Strange Encounter* 15
CHAPTER 3. *Edward* 29
CHAPTER 4. *Getting in Deeper* 36
CHAPTER 5. *Remnants of Pisa* 42
CHAPTER 6. *Leaving London* 48
CHAPTER 7. *Introducing Trelawny* 57
CHAPTER 8. *Slamming the Door* 68
CHAPTER 9. *Soirée with Thornton* 73
CHAPTER 10. *Mrs Dickens Transplanted* 83
CHAPTER 11. *In Confidence* 97
CHAPTER 12. *Solutions* 102
CHAPTER 13. *At Home with Trelawny* 110
CHAPTER 14. *Plans* 119
CHAPTER 15. *Beyond her wildest dreams* 125
CHAPTER 16. *Firenze* 131
CHAPTER 17. *Letters from Home* 139
CHAPTER 18. *If Music be the Food of Love...* 144
CHAPTER 19. *The Villa Dorsini* 150
CHAPTER 20. *Art and Love* 158
CHAPTER 21. *Challenges* 162
CHAPTER 22. *'She never told her love...'* 167
CHAPTER 23. *Reality* 171
CHAPTER 24. *La Scala* 176
CHAPTER 25. *Changes* 180
CHAPTER 26. *Mrs Dickens' Surprise* 190
CHAPTER 27. *Boundaries* 194
CHAPTER 28. *Freedom* 198
CHAPTER 29. *Simply Pleasure* 204
CHAPTER 30. *1872* 208
A FINAL NOTE 213

ABOUT THE AUTHOR

Coreen Turner held senior posts in further education, finally as principal of a sixth form college, but managed to keep alive the fire of literature lighted for her by an inspirational teacher. She is fascinated by literary houses and the aspects of biography which fill the gaps between the facts, the 'what ifs' that lurk in everyone's life. She is now working on a novel about Julia Hunt's brother, Thornton. She lives in Stratford upon Avon.

This story is based on real people and events.

'All the imagination needs is the stimulus of facts.'
– Barry Unsworth, *'Losing Nelson'*, *1999.*

INTRODUCTION

Julia Trelawny Hunt was born in 1826 and appears in censuses, memoirs and music archives. She was a talented musician, a daughter of the poet and journalist Leigh Hunt, whom Charles Dickens satirizes unpleasantly in *Bleak House*. Her beauty and talent are well recorded. Letters from her father to her survive in the Leigh Hunt archive, adding flesh to the bones of her skeleton biography. She died unmarried in 1872, in her own lodgings, a single woman with an independent life. The gaps between the facts reveal her journey to independence and her story will resonate with any woman who has experienced poverty, lack of opportunity and the maternal instinct which enriches and complicates their lives.

CHAPTER 1

Uninvited Guests

London glows in the sky as darkness falls; two shadowy figures in Tavistock Square Gardens rustle and crackle; the woman swears softly as she pulls her dress away from the clinging brambles.

'Henry!' Her voice is whispering, urgent. 'Help me!'

This is Julia Trelawny Hunt, daughter of James Henry Leigh Hunt, radical journalist and Harold Skimpole in Dickens' novel, *Bleak House*. Julia herself is Comedy in the same novel. Henry is her good natured brother, drawn into her frequent scrapes through his devotion.

London in the 1850s. From the foliage of the trees around them rain drips; the London fogs are at their height and the smell is sooty and acrid. Through the leaves extravagant light beams from a house at the corner of the square; a thin horse clops by, knowing its route better than the sleepy hunched coachman. Skinny children hover outside the grand house, scratching in the fallen leaves for coins dropped by customers tipping hackney drivers, desperate to clear a path for expected visitors and eat before they sleep. Voices and laughter float from the glowing windows.

Henry, extricating himself from thorns a few yards from her, gives a final tug and lands by her side, smiling down from a willowy height at his little sister. The Hunt children are all sorts of shapes and sizes, and these two bear each other little resemblance, except for the black bright eyes and olive complexions which betray the American Indian blood of their father. Julia often wonders whether their dark skins possibly come from a slave or a native Barbadian. She once heard her father and Elizabeth Barrett Browning discussing the origins of their dark skins, and Hunt saying later to her mother that presumably the poet's tyrannical father's opposition to his children's marrying was because he feared black blood emerging. Well, she thinks, he should know... Henry is humming the opening bars of the overture to *The Marriage of Figaro*; she joins in as she tugs impatiently, tearing her trapped taffeta skirt near the hem with a sharp little rasp.

'Damn!' and she laughs.

'I wish you wouldn't,' says Henry tolerantly. 'Try to be a nice girl. Nice girls don't swear. It's quite fun for me to be seen with the most dangerous woman in town, even if she is my sister, but you really shouldn't swear.' He folds the billowing skirt over his arm and with the other one helps her out of the tangle. She jumps on to the grass and stands laughing in front of him, small, dark, bright, black-eyed, her mixed colourful clothes hiding the poverty that results in an eclectic mix of borrowing and buying second hand where she can. The result, though, is startling, attractive and mysterious; at twenty-nine she is single but sought after. They have been hiding in the gardens for a perfect moment to make their presence felt.

They leave the tangled undergrowth and make their way towards the fine house on the corner, Charles Dickens' new statement of his prosperity. Henry hesitates, brushing down his respectable, shabby clothes, but Julia advances fearlessly and positions herself by the gate.

'Is this wise?' he asks gently.

'I hate him,' she says cheerfully. 'I really hate him. He owes us a dinner at least. I will never, never forgive him for what he did to Papa in that book[1]; and to include Mary, Jacintha and me!' Closing her eyes, she quotes from memory, unable to erase it. '"This," said Mr Skimpole, "is my beauty daughter, Arethusa - plays and sings odds and ends like her father. This is my Sentiment daughter, Laura, plays a little but don't sing. This my Comedy daughter, Kitty, sings a little but don't play..."'

'You're cross because he called you Comedy, whereas you'd have preferred to be Beauty, which clearly Mary was, and Jacintha is Sentiment,' interrupts Henry mildly. The appraisal of the sisters is accurate, except for Comedy who, standing before him, is superlatively good at both singing and playing. 'Father took it, why can't you? But he was quite perceptive; as Father says, you never take life seriously!'

'What is there to be serious about, Henry?' Her

---

[1] *Bleak House*: Charles Dickens, 1853.

eyes glitter as she ties her bonnet ribbon into a neat bow with a sharp tug. 'Serious women who think about their futures end up with husbands who reduce them to dependents with no life of their own - you have only to look at our own dear family, and certainly Mr Dickens'.' She broke off. 'Oh, come on, for goodness sake! There's no time to talk about seriousness. If we don't hurry up and sing we're unlikely to get invited in to dinner and I'm starving - really starving.'

Henry shrugs good naturedly; he knows better than to argue with Julia on these issues. She plants her feet equally, breathing deeply and positioning her hands elegantly in front of her firm breasts. They start to sing the duet of Susanna and Figaro from the opening of *The Marriage of Figaro*, her perfect soprano and his very good baritone rising mellifluously into the night air. Little birds, shivering on bare branches, abandon their sleepy twittering and fall silent as these competitors gather strength. Henry was born in Italy and imbibed his music from the Italian voices he heard all around him in Lord Byron's villa, when his parents lived with him while their father and Byron edited an English journal. Julia has learned songs from Henry and passionately regrets that she was born in London after their parents returned to England. But she has risen above this disadvantage by becoming the best singer and pianist in the Hunt stable, and indeed in London amateur, and some professional circles. As their voices are carried on the night air the lighted windows scrape open, flung up by eager listeners: very quickly, figures are silhouetted and voices float down praising, enquiring. The song dies, and after a pause the door opens and a servant comes languidly to the railings to speak with them.

'Mr Dickens presents his compliments,' he says pointedly to Henry, ignoring Julia as if she were a woman of the streets, 'and,' he sniffs, 'begs you to come in and sing to his company. There will be some reward.'

'Thank you,' says Julia abruptly, imperiously, before Henry can respond, pulling herself up to her full height, a little short of five feet two. 'We will come in for the reward but we need dinner as well. Please see that Mr Dickens understands.' The manservant narrows his eyes, looking waspishly at her. He has seen better days when serving a minor duke and finds the new money of the Dickens, their habits and their friends, hard to bear. Turning, he indicates sharply with his head that they should follow him. Julia goes first, pulling a long, pompous face at Henry behind the servant's back, her tongue just behind her lips. They enter a prettily tiled hallway; she swings her cloak from her shoulders, narrowly missing the hothouse flowers reflected in a huge, gilded mirror. Henry catches it neatly, adds his own and his hat to it, and waits for the manservant to take them from him. The man sighs. Julia removes her bonnet, her dark hair gleaming in the golden light provided by the lavish beeswax sconces. She smooths her dress, looks down and examines the result, then confidently mounts the stairs, Henry following in her wake.

Julia is exhilarated by the noise above; she can't wait to enter the hot room and see who the company is. She knows they have been performing Wilkie Collins' play, *The Frozen Deep*, for many of the amateur

JULIA'S SHILLING

actors are her family's friends, and word gets round when Dickens is having one of his jolly evenings, with friends and hangers on assembled to praise. She stands in front of Henry - she wishes he was not so deferential - and sweeps the room with her dark, intelligent eyes. Everything in the room is new and somewhat shiny, so different from her parents' and siblings' homes, where treasured pieces of frail furniture gather dust with ancient paintings thick with smoke, and busts of poets carried to and from the Mediterranean, chipped but glorious. Through the thick pall of cigar smoke and the fog which has billowed in from the opened windows, she discerns familiar faces: Wilkie Collins, of course, and the great author himself, and some of his many children; George Henry Lewes, without his paramour George Eliot, Henry Mayhew beside the fireplace, whose work *London Labour and the London Poor* Dickens regularly plunders for his novels; the usual adoring stage struck ladies, including, she recalls, one very important to Dickens; other family members, and there in a corner, mountainous, weary, apprehensive and exhausted, Catherine Dickens. Julia ignores the others and goes straight to her, sinking into a low chair in a rustle of taffeta and silk.

'Julia! I'm so pleased you're here! I didn't realise Charles had invited you! I would have been looking forward to it all evening if I had!'

Julia pulls an apologetic face. 'He didn't. But Henry and I had heard you had goings on this evening and we often sing outside in the hope of a little money or a dinner and generally we are not disappointed. So we tried our luck - and it's worked.' She leans closer to

Mrs Dickens. 'And you? How are you?' She takes the older woman's white chubby hand, notes how deeply the wedding ring bites into the flesh, and encloses it in her own. 'I told Mama we might gain entrance to your palace and she begs to be remembered.'

Catherine sighs, the clear light from a nearby paraffin lamp revealing the deep lines around the mouth and eyes. She greatly prefers candlelight, softer and more flattering; in this light she feels aware of everything Charles has said about her fading looks, her gathering flesh; she is sure everyone in the room sees her deficiencies too. What a relief it is to have this dear girl near to her to mask her unease.

'That's good,' she whispers, apprehensive of her watchful husband's ears and eyes; apprehensive too because present is the lovely Miss Ternan, rightfully there because she is a professional actress playing in *The Frozen Deep*, respectably there because accompanied by her actress mother. Catherine had only recently had a bracelet intended for Miss Ternan wrongly returned to her by a puzzled jeweller. The arguments that had generated seemed now to be out of control; carpenters had arrived to raise an excluding partition in the Dickens' bedroom to add fuel to the myth that their marriage had always been unhappy; Dickens' threats of separation seem ever closer.

'That's good,' she repeats, softly. 'Is she well? I haven't seen her since the Skimpole... incident.'

'Not surprising,' laughs Julia, her good temper as ever surmounting her bitterness. 'Yes, she's well, but mainly confined to bed and a little dependent on - medication - of sorts.' She smiles. 'You know - you've had ten children and so has she. Loving them doesn't make your insides right, does it? A little help is needed!'

Mrs Dickens chuckles, amused by the younger woman's candour. 'You'll find out, sadly, my dear. It's the price we pay for security, and the satisfaction of having our beautiful children.' She raises her eyes briefly, scanning the room for these loved objects, then drops them quickly again as they almost meet her husband's. Looking fondly at Julia she says, 'Are you going to marry that nice young painter?'

Julia giggles. 'No, no, no. Despite being twenty-nine I love my music and although living among my relatives irks me at times, I'm ready to put up with it for my freedom!' She gestures dramatically with outstretched arms, accidentally thumping the elegantly frock- coated back of Mr Dickens who is hovering near, trying to hear the conversation. Catherine's plump smooth face, framed by her pale hair, betrays nervousness, eyes flickering from Julia to her husband, who keeps a steady eye on them both. He suspects subversion from Julia, and has caught most of the words. That family has been reared with revolution in their blood. He doesn't want his soon-to-be discarded wife to get any ideas about freedom; he needs to break it up.

He turns with affected surprise at the accidental thump; Julia rises from her seat and curtseys low, spreading her rustling skirts skilfully, apologising with an ironic smile.

'Well, Julia, is it time for a song? My guests have exhausted themselves with their dramatics and will welcome relaxation!'

Julia stands firmly before him. The room smells of the food previously served, wafting in from the contiguous dining room; it mingles with the sooty smell of the glowing coal fires, the scent on the women, the sweat of the men in their high collars and studs. She is very hungry, in a way that most of those present have never experienced. If they eat before singing, they are sure of the meal; it will be hotter, with greater choice, before the servants have started on it. Dickens is looking at her with barely concealed dislike; he has never been able to manage witty, proud women, except for the rich, admiring ones, and here he has this offspring of radicalism, known throughout London for her beautiful voice, her vivacity and, more threatening, her challenging views. Julia considers; she can't sing on a full stomach, she has warmed up since entering the overheated room. Henry, leaning against the fine marble fireplace, watches from under his long dark lashes to see what she will do. He always follows her lead.

'Of course,' she replies smoothly, 'we'll sing now. What would you like? We can do Mozart, Bellini and the very latest Verdi. Always up to date, the Hunts.' Several of the guests urge Dickens towards the Verdi, eager to hear the new arias from Italy. Dickens quickly rearranges his face into a smile, offers Julia his hand, which she refuses, to guide her towards the piano.

'What a fine new instrument,' she says, genuinely loving the glossy wood of the Broadwood, stroking it sensuously with her fingers. 'This is indeed a change from our old piano.' It certainly was, eight octaves instead of five, shining strings and beige felt dampers. 'I need to play a little before we start, to do this lovely creature justice. Do you mind?' Dickens nods his black curly head, and stands back from her, as if she might sting.

Julia settles herself on the padded rotating stool - nothing but the very best in this house - and ripples a few testing arpeggios. Her dark hair gleams, the olive skin on her cheeks and bare shoulders is slightly flushed from the warmth and the occasion. Her supple hands work the keyboard. She quickly draws the guests around her. She plays snatches of Beethoven sonatas, a Chopin mazurka, a burst of Mozart. Then she stops, leans back, satisfied, and Henry comes and stands in the piano's curve, his hand resting on the polished wood. His tall good looks are as pleasing as Julia's diminutive beauty. She smiles up at him, almost professional, correct.

'The Verdi?' He nods. They have been practising a duet from *La Traviata* since they had obtained a battered score from an ancient professor at the Academy; on loan for a night Julia had rapidly copied the music before she returned it, when she went for her lesson. Julia has to accompany as well as sing on this demanding new instrument with its shades and colours and complicated pedals; she is stretched to her limits. Henry, however, has a baritone which gives a burnish to her beautiful soprano and he does not let her down, sensing her nervousness, with this instrument, the new music, this company and in this house under the eye of the man who has so betrayed their family in his novel. He waits for her, senses from her breathing that she is ready, and their voices combine exquisitely in what proves to be a better acoustic than the cold pavement. They finish to an emotional silence, and it is a second or two before the applause starts. She remembers her father saying that a pause before applause is a true measure of the audience being moved. She keeps her smooth head down and when the applause breaks, plus the odd 'Brava!', she knows how well they have succeeded. Henry lifts her from the stool with outstretched hand and she curtseys prettily. 'Encore!' rings out, and smiling at Henry she gives him the signal that they should do their Italian songs, shorter, lighter.

Half an hour later, exhausted by repeated requests, they finally, hands on their hearts, finish the recital. It has been good. They have been good. They move into the centre of the room, Henry to talk to one of the Dickens' sons, Julia returning to Catherine Dickens, who spreads an inviting hand to the seats empty on either side of her. Julia is not unaware of the empty seats; it is as if the present company is nervously considering its chances as the rumours circulate about the Dickens' marriage and Miss Ellen Ternan. Husband or wife? Which side to be on? She is about to sit down when the husband bears down upon her, seizing her hand so that she is jerked upright. She looks at him furiously. Catherine's face is taut with anxiety.

'Julia,' he says firmly, 'you are hungry, bring Henry and come next door to eat.' She is propelled with a hand in her back, she shudders slightly, and finds herself in the greatly over decorated dining room. The sight of the remains of the lavish food nearly overwhelms her and she has to restrain herself not to fall on it and gobble, crush it into her mouth. She turns to Dickens.

'And the reward? It was promised. It is our fee. You know only too well the circumstances of our family, after all you depicted our poverty so accurately, so vividly in *Bleak House.*' Her black eyes beneath their darkly arched brows meet his unfalteringly; he drops

JULIA'S SHILLING

his. He sighs heavily.

'Will you never leave it alone, you wilful girl?' he whispers. 'I have spoken to your father and that should be an end to it.'

'No,' she whispers back, mockingly, putting her head quite close to his, 'I won't, for it will last against our family as long as your works are read. As long as they buy you all this' - and she gestures scornfully at the sparkling chandeliers, polished furniture and pretty glass - 'and possibly when you're dead. Just give me the fee, then we'll eat and be gone, and not disturb your fragile conscience any more.'

He catches his breath, then lets it go slowly. At least there are no witnesses to his confusion, for confused he is; he is used to respect, deference, adulation from women, not the opinionated, fearless sharpness of this young baggage. He understands what fires her venom: he regrets it a little, but it added to the story and caused much comment, boosting sales amongst the curious. Just get rid of her, he thinks. Turning to an elaborately carved bureau used for housekeeping purposes, he takes his heavy key ring from an inner pocket and unlocks it, extracting a small leather bag and takes from it with a jingle two glinting sovereigns. He holds them out to her, hoping she will find the hard cash insulting. Instead, she smiles broadly, revealing her good white teeth.

'Make it guineas,' she says. There is a sharp intake of breath from Henry, isolated by the door during this exchange. Feeling in his little bag, Dickens produces two more coins, his face murderous. She takes them quickly, challengingly dropping them down her cleavage for want of a more convenient place.

'You can leave us to eat now and return to your guests,' she says lightly. 'Goodnight, Mr Dickens.' Dismissed like a servant in his own house, Dickens leaves, every bone expressing outrage.

Henry shakes his head and lets out the long breath he has been holding. 'How you dare...'

'Eat, my dear, eat,' Julia interrupts, 'as much as you can as fast as you can, before he has a change of mind.' They pile fish, meat, vegetables on to plates, eating as they go; Julia has not eaten since breakfast when she shared a small portion of his favourite porridge and a nectarine with her father. She scoops the coins from between her breasts.

'Two guineas!' she laughs, 'two guineas! When did I last hold so much money? Do you want some, or shall I take it straight back to the aged parents? Food and fuel, and rum for Mama!'

'Take it,' he replies. 'When you've some change I could do with a few shillings for boots for the boys, they grow so fast, but for now, take it.' He smiles at her, pleased at her pleasure and with their success, admiring her boldness, her courage and, he must admit, her downright insolence. Only she, he reflects, could get away with it. He goes in search of their cloaks, which Julia twitches quickly away from the manservant with a haughty nod. Without waiting for him to open the door for them, she grabs the handle, seizes Henry's hand and disappears into the night as if the devil himself were at her heels.

CHAPTER 2

A Strange Encounter

They walk rapidly away from the square and strike southbound for an omnibus route, Julia skipping to keep up with Henry's long stride. He almost carries her along, so glad is he to leave the dangers of Tavistock House. Julia and Mrs Dickens, Julia and Charles Dickens, Catherine and Charles Dickens - these stresses and tensions are not compatible with Henry's genial and tolerant nature. Julia starts to cough as the foggy night air invades her small frame. He stops, an arm around her shoulders; her cough is hollow, rasps a little in her throat. There is no phlegm rattling in her lungs which would indicate a winter ailment; would that it did. His smooth forehead wrinkles with anxiety.

'I'm all right now,' she gasps, leaning against him. 'Don't look so worried, dear boy! It's just singing for so long in that overheated room. I'm not used to being that warm. And the coal fires give off such fumes!' One last cough and she pulls herself together, wrapping her cloak tightly around her. 'Are you going home now? Dina will be missing you, and the children. Thank you for coming with me. I'd never have gone in alone.'

'Really? I doubt that: my fearless sister?'

'Not entirely fearless. That man still has the power to unsettle me.' They are standing in a pool of gaslight near to a tree, fast shedding its leaves, not yet crisp underfoot. Traffic rumbles past, coaches, hackney carriages, omnibuses, a lone rider speeding through the night. Suddenly Julia looks tired.

'I'm going on the bus, opposite way from you. We'd better get going, not miss the last one.' Henry has to visit his brother nearby. They hear horses approaching, harness jingling, snorting nostrils, sharp hooves on the new road surface.

'That's yours,' cries Julia, and waves the swaying bus down.

'Are you seeing Edward?' he asks.

She gives him a swift kiss, says, 'No, not tonight,' and he leaps aboard, mounting the stairs to sit on the knifeboard, waving as the horses pull away. She waves extravagantly back, then crosses the road to be prepared for her bus when it heaves into sight. She sits down on some steps by a horse trough, relieved to be at rest and not to have to respond to Henry's solicitude. She leans back and closes her eyes, putting her hand into the silky internal pocket of her full skirt, to feel the luxury of those sovereigns and shillings; her hand meets some cold fingers, colder than hers. She screams and leaps up.

'What are you *doing*?' she shouts to a bundle of rags, vainly trying to extricate its fingers from hers. Her strong pianist's hand keeps hold of a skinny wrist, and she swings the bundle round to face her. In the dark it is not easy to see what she has hold of: tattered cloth, a cap bigger than its owner's head, no easily visible face - she draws the form towards her to try to see a face but in the poor light nothing can be seen. She realises that it is blotted out by the grime in every feature.

'What are you *doing*?' she repeats, surer now of her captive and that her money is still in her hanging pocket. She is left holding a thin, dirty wrist and is not sure of her next move. The child, for child it is, is presumably male from the tattered trousers slung about a bony frame. 'Come on, what were you doing, you little thief!' The child tries to pull away but she pulls hard down and he cannot. He croaks hoarsely.

'Let me go, lady, I ain't got nothing from you, let me go!' He wriggles but she is a good match for him.

'What's your name?'

'What d'you want to know for? I ain't taken nothing and I ain't going to no police. I'll kill you first!' Julia surveys the trembling bundle before her and laughs, coughing taking over from laughter and finally silencing her. The boy starts to cough too, and she keeps hold of him until he stops.

'Never mind the police. What *is* your name?'

A single gruff syllable.

'Tom.'

Julia can now see the whites of his eyes; huge, probably brown eyes, darting around Julia, looking for an escape. She draws him back to the steps and makes him sit down. There is nothing of him: the rags flutter in the light breeze, the arms are stick thin, uncovered; similar legs protrude from the half-mast trousers. There are no shoes; a child's feet worn to an old man's by the pavements and the cold. She thinks of the delicious chubbiness of Henry's children's feet.

'Where do you live?'

'What d'you want to know for?'

'I might go and see your parents and tell them that you tried to rob a lady. That you're becoming a skilled pickpocket, that I could have lost all my hard earned money.'

Tom laughs. 'You can't do that,' he says, letting her release his hand but somehow compelled to sit down with her. 'We ain't got no parents. So there.'

'What's happened to them?' Julia replies coolly, not wishing to be taken for a ride.

'Me dad fell from a scaffold in the new house building. Me mum took us into the workhouse,' - a shadow passed over the grimy features - 'and then she died, then me two little brothers, and now there's just Janey and me.'

Julia persists. 'But you can't still be in the workhouse, people from there are not allowed out.'

'We - er - left,' he says quietly, 'they separated us and we're brother and sister and it wasn't right. So we left, escaped, I suppose you'd call it. Better to be together.' Julia understood that perfectly. Her siblings are everything to her.

'So is - Janey - at home now?'

'We don't have no 'ome. We 'ad a room but got behind with the rent. Now we go to a lodging 'ouse for a penny if we've got one, we take it in turns to sleep there, but I don't like her on the streets on 'er own at night, there's bad people about; but there's often worse in the lodging house.' He stopped, as if overwhelmed by the insolubility of the problem. He turns to face Julia. 'What are you going to do?' he asks in a weary voice. He feels he should probably run for it, but he quite likes this woman, talking to her, not a thing he does often to an adult. Julia thinks of the two guineas in her pocket; there is great need in the Hunt household for this money, for essentials and, she had hoped, the odd luxury. But she loves children and although her nephews and nieces are not sumptuously catered for, they are clothed, warm, educated to reasonable standards, and loved. This child is hungry enough to steal, clothed in rags, cold, unhoused. Vulnerable. In danger from predators. She sighs.

'I'm going to give you a shilling.' She knows she should probably give pence but that is how Dickens gave her the money. The boy's eyes widen. 'If I give it to you will you spend it on clothes or lodgings or food? No gambling or penny gaffs?' He gives a scoffing shake of the head.

'I'd never spend money like that,' he croaks scornfully. 'Only a fool 'd do that and I'm not a fool!' Julia thinks about this and says, although reluctantly in case it embarrasses him, 'Can you read or write?'

He almost smiles at her. 'Course I can!' he says proudly. 'We've not always been like this. When me dad was alive we 'ad money and he paid a penny a week for us all to go to school. When he died Mum could only work enough to get food and pay the rent, but she had a bad cough and when she couldn't work no more that's when we went in the workhouse. 'Ave you ever been in one, miss?' he says in a rush of confidentiality. 'It's like prison, and you're all separated, and the food's terrible, and the boring work drives you mad.' Julia shudders. There had been many dark times in the Hunt household; constant debt and indebtedness, frequent house moves to save a guinea on the rent, all having root in the long ago fine and imprisonment imposed on her father, Leigh Hunt, and his brother, John, before Julia and Henry were born; all testament to their father's radical beliefs and good conscience, but the foundation of a lifetime's embarrassed poverty.

'No,' she says quietly, 'I haven't ever been in one.'

'Why you giving me a shilling, miss? You don't look rich like some ladies,' he added, for the first time looking at her closely and recognising her twice-turned gown, a procedure he knows from earlier days when his mother worked at sewing. 'You might need it. Not that I don't want it,' he adds brightly.

The street is quieter now, fewer vehicles, and Julia realises that the receding lanterns swaying away from her are on the last omnibus to Hammersmith. Her conversation had so engrossed her she had failed to see it approach and so had not hailed it. How is she to get home? But first things first.

'Here is the shilling,' she says, groping in her pocket. 'I want you to share it with your sister and use it wisely. Let her choose what is most important to her.' She places the precious object in the outstretched grimy palm. 'Put it somewhere safe, there's pickpockets about,' and she smiles at him; there is a pause before he realises she's made a joke, but then he chuckles.

'All right, miss, and thank you ever so much. Why are you giving it me?' he asks again, still puzzled.

'Because you need it,' she replies, 'and I want to see you again. Will you meet me here in a week's time? In the morning? Early? Can you work out a week?'

'Course I can!' He is fairly outraged at her assumption, but she knows how the poor live. 'I'll be here, and I'll bring Janey!' As if mistrusting his luck, he suddenly pulls away into the shadows and vanishes.

Julia is startled. For a moment she doubts he was ever there, but the musty, slightly animal smell he brought with him lingers and convinces her of his reality. She sits on the steps in the gloom; there is less light about as the traffic with its lanterns decreases, and she wonders how to get home. She can walk. She is nearer to Edward than to her father's house, but she sets off towards Hammersmith, muffling her face against the fog. There are few people about and most of them harmless, trying to find somewhere dry to sleep for the night; raucous young men do not bother her, but a group further on do and she regretfully hails a slowly passing cab and takes a cheap returning fare to take her the last mile, eating into the precious earnings. A weary hour later she turns in at the wooden gate in Hammersmith and, entering her father's parlour, she kisses him lightly as he peers short-sightedly at his book in the light of a single candle. His upturned face is remarkably beautiful, brilliant black eyes and dark skin emphasised by his long white hair. He rakes the dying embers of the tiny fire and the sparks fly upward. She is home and he is happy.

***

Julia sits in the dying light in the kitchen, peering at the pattern she has cut from the old cotton drawers and camisoles which are about to be relegated to household cleaning. Most women wear drawers now, except her mother, who regards them as unnecessary encumbrances, absent in her youth. These are tiny and tricky, for Henry's children, and her eyes, usually sharp, struggle with the fine stitching in the poor light. She stands up, sighs, and, stretching her arms above her head to ease her aching shoulders, reaches into the candle box and lights another from the guttering one, placing it in a battered silver candle stick, blackened by time and infrequent cleaning. Returning to her task, she is suddenly aware of her father in the room; he glides about so quietly she is often surprised by his sudden appearances; he stops by the table and peers closely at the little garments and chuckles.

'So tiny, such little angels...'

'Come, come, Papa, you know they're little terrors really!'

'You're a good girl to help Dina, my dear, I don't know what Henry and she would do without your help...' He loves the strong bonds between his children. His beautiful voice falters as he eases himself into the only other chair which creaks very gently as he lowers his slight frame into it. He really should eat more, she thinks, all this nonsense about only eating fruit and little else because that's what he did in Italy thirty years ago has simply been a cover for the lack of food in the house and his desire over the years to keep his children fed. Now they are grown and gone and he has been awarded a civil pension to honour his work it isn't strictly necessary but he can't break the habit.

'Mama said you were at the Dickens' last night?'

Julia senses his anxiety and burns with resentment. 'Indeed we were,' she says, as casually as possible, leaning across the table to scoop his long white hair back to prevent singeing by the candle, and so she could better see the expression in his black eyes. 'Does that worry you?'

'Not worry, my dear,' he says slowly, his long fingers playing with the base of the candlestick. 'Not worry - exactly - but I hated the Skimpole thing. Didn't realise it myself until my friends told me. Why would he do it? He made me appear deceitful, improvident, my house dirty, my daughters—'

Julia interrupted. 'And you thought he was your friend,' she replies quietly. 'That was the hurt for all of us. But yes. We did go. My idea, not Henry's, so don't be cross with him. I vented my spleen a little, we sang beautifully, his guests may hire us for their parties and I made him pay us two guineas! That's better than worrying about *Bleak House*. And I saw Catherine, who looks utterly miserable as he parades his little actress in front of everyone and pretends there's nothing in it—'

'Whoa!' said her father, as if steadying a runaway horse. 'I'm sure he wouldn't behave improperly—'

'Papa! He's no different from any other man. His writing needs a perfect home life to sell *Household*

Words, so he'll hush up any scandal and Catherine will be the loser. Women are.'

'You'll feel differently once you're married,' Leigh counters, patting the back of her hand as she busies herself with the needle, stabbing the material as if Mr Dickens himself were on the kitchen table. 'Your mother and I have been so happy—'

'If I could find a man like you that might be different,' she says firmly, giving a twist to the cotton and snapping it off as if it lived, 'but if we're being frank, Papa, even your married bliss and children have taken its toll on Mama. She's confined upstairs, dependent on brandy and rum to get through the day, you love her devotedly but have little life with her now—'

He stands up, moves towards the meagre fire which burns to heat the little oven, and spreads his ink stained, opaque hands to gather a little warmth.

Julia continues. 'Her body is wrecked by having ten children, her mind is addled by the laudanum she took to get through the day with all of us needing feeding and clothing, and her constant anxiety about money. She loved you and backed your radical politics and writing despite the poverty they brought. I remember people made fun of her when we were children because she borrowed things and didn't return them; she couldn't, she had nothing to return. All the love in the world that you gave her, and we did too, hasn't been able to save her from her decline.'

Leigh sits again as if blown down by the vehemence of Julia's speech. Pulling his silk cape around his shoulders for warmth he replies quietly,

JULIA'S SHILLING

'It's hard to admit but you're almost right. When I shared our poor home with Shelley and Keats when they were in need I thought little of the added burden it put on your mother...' Julia drops her work and raises a hand to stop him.

'It's in the past, Pa. You can't live with regrets. She loved - loves - you and she made life as good as she could for all of us. Let's just deal with what we have now, which is two sovereigns, I've eaten into the shillings; I took a cab and I gave one away.' She kept her eyes firmly on the thread she was pulling as she said this. Her father raised a quizzical, unsurprised eyebrow. 'A little boy - he was starving and had a sister...'

'I believe you, *cara Giulia*; it has always amused me how my family having very little themselves, ally themselves with the poor. We are not really poor; we can work, and we get manna from heaven from time to time. But you need shoes badly - have you thought about that?'

'I'm thinking of getting boots! The women in the Langham Place group wear Balmoral boots and wear their skirts ankle length to deal with the filth in the streets.' That did shake her father.

'Not short skirts, Julia, not while you're still unmarried,' he says firmly. 'We'll never get you a husband.'

'Don't want a husband, I've told you so often before. Happy to love my nieces and nephews, goodness knows I see enough of them to feel they are my own, and I'll take my chances with my men friends. I'm not short of company.'

'That's true,' Leigh says, quite severely. 'I thought Edward wanted to marry you, and he'd be a good provider, he's a good family friend, almost a relation through Jacintha's marriage—'

'Yes. He does want to. But isn't it about what *I* want too?' She gathered up the little garments and folded them away into a dilapidated linen basket. 'How could I go out singing and teaching if I was married to Edward and pregnant all the time?'

'But you wouldn't have to—'

'But I'd *want* to!' She almost shouts. 'I'd want to! Music is the only thing I've been able to do well, to scavenge and improve on out of young ladies' so-called accomplishments. The rest of my education is almost as bad as the other silly women I meet. But now there's people trying to get colleges going so that women can go to university like their brothers; that's what they really talk about at Langham Place, not short skirts and Balmoral boots. I'm too old now but I might still benefit at the fringes, I might even contribute. They're trying to get a Working Women's College started to go alongside the Men's. All the teachers are volunteers - I could teach music.' She pauses, looks very directly at her father. 'Anyway, you don't need me to produce babies, there's lots of your wonderful genes distributed already. And do I want just Edward for the rest of my life?'

Leigh sighs. She was right about his genes; Thornton, his eldest, has nine children distributed across two families; the others have single families, fewer children, but all struggled to keep them fed clothed and educated, mostly through their pens. Writing was certainly in the genes, and music. He had taught Julia to play the piano and when she had proved so gifted he managed to pay from time to time at the new Academy. Between times it was her own assiduity and talent which turned her in to the remarkable musician she now is. She breaks into his reverie.

'I'm going out now,' she says, gathering a few articles which lie around the untidy kitchen - a hairbrush and flannel by the old wash stand, a wispy cotton gown, a shawl, light slippers, several sheets of music - and bundles them into a carpet bag. It is a handsome, well-worn object of which she was justly proud: when she had been to sing at a soirée with some of the Langham Place group she had sung some American songs which her father, who knew them from his childhood, had taught her. This had pleased Dr Blackwell who had qualified as a doctor in New York. These wealthy women were agitating for women's education and were sympathetic to any woman who was trying to improve herself, and that certainly included Julia. They admired her talent and radical ancestry while regretting her poverty, and helped where they could. Julia's modest fees were always promptly paid and they often passed on helpful items, clothes, sheet music and recently this bag. Dr Blackwell had used it in America and when Julia naively admired it, handed it over with huge grace and thanks for the trouble she had taken with the American songs.

'I'm going to Edward's so you should be pleased as you clearly regard him as good son-in-law material.' She giggles. 'I'm not sure how he regards you! But I shan't be back tonight, so I'll do Mama before I go and you must look after her later on.' Leigh struggles with this news, not the caring for his wife but Julia's absence overnight.

'Are you sure you should stay at the studio, dearest? You will be—'

'Careful? Of course, Papa, how do you think Mr Lewes and George Eliot manage to work all the time and have no children? Clearly Mr Lewes was very fertile before he took up with her. They are, as you would put it, careful. A pity you don't worry about Thornton so much, but I suppose he's a man and that's different...' Her voice falters as she pushes more things into her bag and considers this. She disappears into the tiny scullery where the daily maid, Molly, has left a tray with something unappetising on it, and brings it through. 'Give this to Mama at about six o'clock. I'm going to take her some tea now and tidy her up.' This phrase was a Hunt euphemism for making Marianne wash her hands and face and comb her hair and whatever else she could be persuaded to do. Daughters and daughters-in-law, Hunt himself, share this unenviable task not welcomed by Marianne. Julia carries a small bowl and towel up the stairs. Hunt could hear a murmur of conversation as she busies herself with her mother. He smiles; all is well.

A clattering of feet down the stairs brings Julia back to him. She picks up her cloak and bag and stands on tip-toe to kiss him on the top of his head. Her black eyes gleam and his reflect back.

'Don't worry about me. I'll probably see you tomorrow. Don't wait up!' And closing the cottage front door firmly, she whisks away to catch the omnibus.

CHAPTER 3

Edward

Stepping neatly over the steaming pile the omnibus' horses have left, Julia starts her trek to Hatton Garden. Edward Johnson's studio is within the engraver William Linton's complex; Linton has been a friend of her father for years and their radical activist politics gave them many happy evenings until the Hunts moved to Hammersmith and Linton to Canada. The rambling ancient building is still inhabited by the wood-engravers and painters who once clustered around Linton for his skills and politics. The rickety outside stairs are unlighted and she struggles as her bag swings heavily against her body. A rat scuttles, hurtling towards its squeaking offspring. She is aiming for a strip of yellow light which shines from under a door at the top of the stairs; breathless from climbing too fast, she raps three times then leans against the stair's newel post, breathing deeply.

'Julia?' The door opens and a tall young man, curly brown hair hiding his face, leans out towards her. She can see only his outline against the light in the room; she laughs.

'Were you expecting anyone else?'

He leans forward and takes her bag, then her arm, and draws her into the dimly lighted room. It is a tumble of wood shavings, spilled ink, discarded drawings, a work bench piled high with engravings finished and in progress. Edward Johnson does wood engravings for the *Illustrated London News*, with hard weekly deadlines which keep him late in the studio. But the room has also an air of temporary domesticity, the overstuffed sofa with its shawls and rugs, the coal fire warming the raw night, a coffee pot bubbling against the fire, bread and cheese available for both occupant and scuttling vermin should they want it. He pulls her towards the paraffin lamp, gazing at her tenderly and, holding her head in both his hands, kisses her slowly.

'Why are you so late?' he murmurs, pulling the damp curls away from her forehead and untying her bonnet.

'Oh, Papa, Mama, my nieces' underclothes,' she replies, gently pushing him away and hurrying to the fire. She crouches before it; she is very, very cold, her clothes are too thin for wearing in London fogs and rain; she pulls off the worn gloves and withdraws her stiff fingers, spreading them to the flames, which are now crackling and spitting from the wood spirals Edward has gathered from the floor and added, following with a shovelful of coal. She pulls back from the unaccustomed warmth, the sudden burst of light softening her frozen features. Edward sits beside her on the threadbare turkey rug which partly covers the floor, and rubs her aching, cold back. With him at the back and the fire at the front she is almost comfortably warm.

'You can't go on like this,' he murmurs, unpinning her shining dark hair. 'You're breathing like wheezy bellows.'

'Thank you!'

'A very small, sweet pair,' he picks just such a pair, wooden framed with rivetted skin like a drum, from beside the stove and playfully wheezes them at her, 'but a singer needs good lungs and yours are not what they were.' She sighs and takes his hand from her shoulders and lays it flat on her chest, now rising and falling more gently.

'I'm better. It's temporary. When I start to sing I forget it, so it's probably all in my head. Papa is a hypochondriac, Mama a chronic invalid, perhaps I'm a hysteric?'

Edward laughs exasperatedly. 'You're not. Totally sane. If we get married I could look after you, feed you proper meals, stop you singing outside in the cold.'

'I don't much, only when I need to as an advertisement. Edward, dear heart, you're too good,' she takes his hands between hers and holds them tight. 'But we've said all this before. I don't need looking after, yes I like being loved but that's different; and I have Papa and Mama to look after, the others help but you know I'm the spinster daughter who makes their lives possible since Vincent died.' A shadow passes across her face. 'Papa loved him more than any of us and he helped with his work, whatever little he can do now. He still needs help. His handwriting is still good, but there's the reading out loud and the posting, and managing the house, such as I do.' She giggles. 'I'm not very good at that, as you know, but somehow they both are washed and dressed and laundered and fed as I whizz in and out between pupils and performances. And...' she paused.

'And?'

'We've also done this before, whether I really want to marry.'

'But, sweetness, that's all nonsense! We love each other, you'd love being married and we'd be able to live in the country at the farm. You know you love being there.'

'As a visitor.'

'Fanny would be there to help with the children, she loves a houseful, it would be perfect!'

Julia sighs. 'You really don't understand, do you?' she says sadly, turning to face him and looking very straight into his brown eyes, trying to bore seriousness into him with her unblinking gaze. 'It's not to do with not loving you, I do, it's to do with not wanting to be someone else's property. Some women these days choose not to marry.'

Edward interrupts. 'They're rich women, the sort you mix with when you sing at their soirées, the Leigh Smiths, and Miss Coutts; don't think your life would be like theirs, they have servants and money. That gives them the leisure to learn, do their good works and keep comfortable houses.' He sounded quite savage. 'You'd have neither; you'd have no money except what you earned, you'd have to live with your brothers and sisters when your parents die; and you'll grow old. Don't assume you'd live a life like your rich friends.'

'You'll be telling me I'll be on the streets next,' says Julia mildly, withdrawing her hands and sitting on them.

'It happens,' replies Edward grimly, 'it happens to seduced servant girls, to seamstresses and milliners who nearly die of cold and overwork, to orphans without siblings with no lodging to go to - a woman without means like you could have a very unhappy end.' She stares at him as if this were a threat.

'But poverty for women shouldn't mean no choice but childbearing and drudgery, just an arrangement to prevent starvation and a lifetime of prostitution within marriage! For that's what it can be!' Edward gazes at her in confusion.

'You're very passionate,' he says slowly. 'But it's not what I'm offering. I'm offering love and peace in a country house with relatives who will support you through your childbearing years.'

'I'd go mad in the country and I really don't want childbearing years.'

'The way you behave with me you'd think that's exactly what you want.' She stands up and gives his handsome face a gentle slap.

'How dare you,' she says equably, 'but you make my point for me. Why should I not enjoy the embraces of one who loves me as much as I love him, without having to sell myself as a housekeeper and bedfellow? If you or your friends want a woman you just take one and pay for her. That's not open to me.

JULIA'S SHILLING

I've seen the results of childbearing: my mother, who has the kindest husband but a body wrecked by bearing ten children, now dependent on alcohol and laudanum, and Catherine Dickens, ten children and a husband who is about to abandon her for an actress. And even the Queen, baby after baby, and rumour has it, she doesn't particularly like them. And at least they're still alive! Think of all those who die bearing the babies, and the men just move on, marry another to bring up the children...' She stops, slightly breathless, and stares into the fire as if within its flames she can see these sad histories there.

'It's no good, Edward. We've known each other for years and you still think I should be like everyone else, exchange sex for security. I want to make my own security, I want to be able to choose - what I do, who I make love with, where I live, who I see. I can sing and teach singing and the piano, I can perform. But now the women in the Langham group are trying to get girls to universities - too late for me but I can try to live a life like the one I might have had if I'd had a better education. Even the women who are trying to get into universities sometimes fail the examinations through sheer ignorance of what to men is basic general knowledge, gathered through going to school, however reluctantly.' She stops, perplexed. Edward pulls himself up and stands, towering over this diminutive inferno.

'You *are* your father's daughter, aren't you?' he says fondly, hugging her to him. 'My simple country childhood is no match for your radical upbringing among the free thinkers of this century. I suppose we don't have to marry; do you want to live together like George Eliot and Mr Lewes?'

'No,' she says quickly, 'they have to, because my big brother Thornton gave Mrs Lewes four babies as they slaked their passion, which Mr Lewes accepted as his, so no divorce, not even with the new Act. More fool him. I want, if I choose, to be alone, childless, absorbed in my music and fulfilled in love. If I starve in the process, so be it. Come to bed, Edward, you look as if you're going to lecture me again,' and she leads him gently towards the ancient sofa and, nestling comfortably into it, pulls his tousled head towards her.

CHAPTER 4

Getting in Deeper

The morning light is weak, thin sunshine which does little to warm the chilly studio with its dead fire. Dressing quickly to avoid the cold that pimples her smooth olive skin, Julia swiftly sluices her hands and face in the bowl standing by the ewer. She pauses and sniffs the water suspiciously: it has a faintly rancid smell as though it has not been recently brought from the well in the yard; no matter, worse things happened at home, and Edward's passion for his work made him unaware of regular housekeeping. She scoops the brush out of her carpet bag and with a few deft, hard strokes she has tamed the black mane, wound it round her hand and pinned it at the nape of her neck. She smiles at herself in the flyblown looking glass on the shelf above the work bench; she looks positively respectable, could even have gone straight to a pupil in respectable house. But she is not going to teach; she has other things to do.

Moving softly towards the door she almost wakes

the sleeping Edward, and freezes beside him for a moment, her breath caught by the Grecian features and tight curls. Oh, the temptations of the flesh, she thinks cheerfully - if he weren't so good looking would I love him so much? His torso is partly revealed by the shawl that covers him, and she stops herself from twitching it aside to see more of his perfect body. No; he would wake and then... she just hasn't the time. She turns the handle of the battered door gently and sends creatures resting in the silence scurrying away. At the bottom of the stairs she adjusts her bonnet against the wind and strikes out hard towards Oxford Street; no expensive cabs, she'll walk today.

Her route takes her past the well-appointed house of one of the Langham Place group ladies, familiar to her from her evenings spent singing at soirées where the condition of women is discussed over a suitably frugal repast - none of the sumptuous fare produced at the Dickens' - and a dish of tea. Julia sings to them, partly to lighten the mood of a sombre evening and partly because Miss Smith is kind enough to employ her. The group publishes a magazine and is trying to develop clerical work for women, so that there is an option other than sewing, millinery and prostitution. Julia is popular with the group; her credentials through her father are excellent, a radical journalist imprisoned (admittedly before Julia was born) for criticising the Prince Regent for his outrageous lifestyle, and her singing is quite glorious. Sometimes her rendering of the arias of Verdi's Violetta are so blushingly passionate that the ladies wonder where it all comes from, but they are glad to see a woman doing what she so clearly enjoys, and pay her well. She often ponders the gulf between their comfortable protected lives and her precarious existence, but her happy spirit does not envy or fear them. She sometimes wryly notes the shifting boundaries between old landed and new money, but since she has neither, dismisses it.

She reaches the steps by the horse trough and looks around covertly; he may not turn up, he certainly may not bring his sister. A tired cab horse drinks thirstily, its ears momentarily pricked with pleasure at the water streaming from its tender hairy lips still encased in the steel bit; the bridle jingles as he shakes his head, scattering droplets in a spray caught by the sun. Julia smiles and moves closer to the pink muzzle, stroking downwards with her cupped hand, and murmuring. The cabbie watches amused; he loves his horse and often regrets the relentless overwork which causes early death and disease, but his own lifespan will be little better. Suddenly Julia feels a tug at her sleeve as she smooths the horse's coat.

'Do you like 'em, miss?' says Tom softly. He is standing behind her, and behind him is a scrap of a girl vainly trying to hide by turning her head away. Her feet too are bare, and the skirt of her tattered frock is shortened by the shreds it has lost, revealing thin, grimy legs blue with cold. Julia turns and laughs with surprise and pleasure.

'I love them,' she says, giving the horse a final pat, 'and how pleased I am to see both of you!'

'Didn't think we'd come, did you,' he sniffs, glaring all of a sudden. 'Thought we couldn't remember the days of the week, didn't you? Thought we was stupid!'

'No, I did not! I thought Janey might be frightened,

coming to meet a strange woman.' She moves towards the girl and takes a skinny cold hand in hers. Janey does not look up, her tired grey eyes searching the ground for some invisible object. 'Tom and I met,' she continues, 'and I thought I'd like to meet you and see if I can help.' God knows how, she is honest enough to think, but I'll try.

Janey is muttering something which Julia can't quite catch.

'She says she doesn't want to be helped if you take her away from me,' Tom falters. 'She's scared without me.'

'Don't be silly,' Julia says briskly, 'why would I want to do that? I want to stop you picking poor women's pockets,' she chuckles, 'because if you don't you'll end up in worse than the workhouse and then you *will* be separated from her.' She looks sideways at Janey, to see if this penetrates. The girl is shaking with cold and fright.

Tom says quietly, 'She's very cold and tired, miss, because we slept out last night.' Before Julia could say anything he rushed on.' We've still got most of the money you gave us, but we couldn't go to the doss 'ouse. It's not safe for her.' He looks away.

'How can it not be safe?' asks Julia suspiciously. 'It must be safer than being on the streets!' He turns to look at her, his pale young face distorted with rage.

'There's men there who go after her - you know - and they make me sleep away from her, not that I *do* sleep, and they try to make her do things and...' Julia took his hand and shook her head to stop him the distress of repeating what she could too well guess;

before long the child would be abducted and sold as a virgin to a brothel where her brother would never see her again.

'If we sleep beneath the bridges it's safer as I'm always there and I'd kill anyone who came near 'er.' He wipes his nose on his sleeve and includes his eyes in the sweeping gesture. 'There's no way out for people like us. Me mum wanted us to be together; she trusted me to look after her, but I'm just not doing it.' His voice breaks and she realises he is weeping, the tears making silvery tracks down his dirty cheeks. Janey moves to put her arms around him.

Julia stands back from them, arms folded, surveying this drooping sculpture of ragged misery. She exhales, blowing out her cheeks and sighing. The girl's shivering is partly cold, but Julia surmises, partly the shock of recent experiences. She doesn't really have time to think, is simply impelled by the raw misery she sees in front of her, and a yearning to make things better for this sad little girl. She can do nothing now; she puts her arms around them both and tries to stop the weeping. Tom recovers and looks murderous, ashamed, defensive. It is beginning to rain and in their thin clothes all three of them need to find shelter.

'Take this,' she says, groping in her pocket for a shilling. 'There must be better places if you can pay a bit more. Go and find somewhere safe for tonight, and meet me tomorrow. I'll have thought it out by then.' Perhaps they won't come; perhaps it will be too late for the girl's safety; perhaps Tom will have committed a crime by then and be detained, and Janey alone. Julia shivers and tries to keep a grip. 'Just come tomorrow. Do you hear?' Her voice rises in her anxiety. Tom nods.

Putting up her shabby umbrella Julia makes for the omnibus for Hammersmith, not for her parents' house but for Henry's. Henry is kindness itself, and weak enough for Julia to manipulate.

CHAPTER 5

Remnants of Pisa

The door is unlocked and Julia enters, calling as she does. The house is a London cottage, close to her parents, still near to countryside but convenient for Henry's work at Somerset House, his day job where he amiably clerks surrounded by similar pleasant young men of reasonably good education and slender means. Henry will not be here, but she knows she will find her sister-in-law, Rosalind in. Their house is less shabby than her parents', and is pleasantly warm, smelling of cooking, untidy commensurate with their four children, one servant and the fact that Dina is near another confinement. She comes through to the hall to greet Julia; they kiss and Julia draws away from her to survey.

'Not twins, I hope?' she laughs. 'Not found out what causes it yet?'

Dina, for so Rosalind has been called since her first lispings in the Italian sun, grimaces and leads her into their drawing room, slightly more than a parlour. A fire burns low in the grate; she stoops stiffly to add coal from the brass hod, pokes it briefly into a flare and lights a candle which illuminates her full cheeks and dark lashes. She subsides into a low chair and rubs her side where her dress strains under its additional occupant. She is a very pretty woman, dark, vivacious but, for the moment, tired. Her links with the Hunts stretch back to Byron and Shelley; she is the daughter of the man with whom Shelley drowned, in the boat broken by a freak, disastrous storm, as they sailed from Pisa to Lerici to join their families. Her parents were in Italy with the poets when the Hunts arrived with their children; Julia not born, Henry a toddler. The two women waited for two men who never arrived; widows in their twenties. All in the past, but a tie like a low current in the water which killed Dina's father and Shelley, and still binds them today.

'You're an awful girl, dear sis,' she says mildly, continuing to massage her expanding figure. 'I know very well what causes it but what's to do? He still loves me and I do so love him. We were never very... practical,' she sighs, 'or we wouldn't have had that poor little soul before we married.'

'For goodness sake!' interrupts Julia. 'We're in the middle of the nineteenth century not the middle ages! You were an ignorant young maiden then, and Henry should have known better. What's to do, say you, many things, from...'

'I know, I know,' Dina interrupts, spreading a preventive hand, 'don't go into detail, the children are all about the place and we can spare them that. Just be sure you take your own medicine for surely as this house always welcomes you it might be difficult to include another mouth.'

Julia looks hard at Dina, whom she loves like a sister. She often stays in her house, earning her keep with the children, whom she also loves, cooking, mending, teaching the little ones their letters and the older ones music. She has a little bed in the girls' room where she knows she can stay whenever she needs a break from her parents, or Edward; this peripatetic life suits her, although it would not many; this way there are not too many eyes or questions. Her musical life with Henry is assured and although hers is the superior talent, he definitely has discrimination and taste. Julia sits on the bulging sofa, her hands together between her knees.

'Would you object so much to another mouth? If you had a contribution from me?'

'Julia! You're not?'

'No, no I'm not! I wouldn't be lecturing you on… whatever,' she says quietly, glancing around to see if any little Hunts have crept into the room. 'It's something quite different.' She tells Dina about Tom and Janey, about the pick pocketing and the threats to their existence. 'They're just children, like yours or Jacintha's, or even Thornton's.' Their eyes meet, fix and laugh nervously at the thought of Julia's brother, Thornton's, many children, legitimate and otherwise. 'But they're terrified and dirty and risk their lives and bodies every night they live on the streets. I wondered if you could help,' she finishes lamely.

Dina leans back, spreading her legs extravagantly, exhaling noisily, feeling the child kicking within her. She is not unsympathetic to Julia's new cause; indeed she often thanks the fates that she has survived despite being the illegitimate child of an unmarried partnership, and wonders what would have happened to her own bastard child with Henry had the baby survived and she not been banished to Paris to stay with Claire Clairmont. Claire, Byron's discarded mistress, was supposed to put Dina off Henry, but encouraged her to follow her heart. So she is not one able to lecture. Her mother, Jane, and Edward Williams had never married, as Jane was still married to the abusing husband she had fled from. Dina has gathered the family she has created since marrying Henry tightly round her, adoring and protecting the children who never hear the word 'no' in their total indulgent freedom, lavishing love on her charming and improvident husband - she tries so hard to keep it all together and does not want to be reminded too much of the perils outside her home. And now, now, she thinks, here is Julia asking her to take into her secure domain two street children? She can all but see the hard won edifice toppling.

Julia waits, without speaking. She is a canny operator who well knows when to speak and when to be silent. Nothing to be gained from impetuosity at this point. A few seconds later Dina says, quite calmly, 'You know I can't bear to see children suffer, but even to help you, my dearest, I don't think I can add two children to this small, single servant house with its limited income. Yes,' she holds up two quite commanding hands and Julia closes her mouth on the suggestion she is about to make, 'I know you would help, as you always do with your nieces and nephews, but I just know I can't do it. I'm too fragile inside. I haven't the capacity to love strangers, only my own. Put it down to never feeling I was loved after we left

Italy. I can love the family I've made, and I love your family. But two strange children? Here?' And she gestured around the room redolent of Hunt music, books, games and hastily abandoned sewing. 'You can't know what it was like after Shelley and my father drowned; Mother so deep in grief she could hardly look at us, coming back to England to God knows where; when I met Henry again later and we fell in love, in a way I was falling in love with the life we had in Italy with your parents and everything still in place. What we've made together here...' her voice falters and Julia realises how close to tears she is, 'what we've made here is precious, and it's precarious, and I won't risk it. And besides, we've so little money.'

Julia knows to go no further. 'My dear,' she says, moving to the floor and sitting in front of Dina so that both of them are caught in the rosy glow of the fire as the coals shift, 'dear Dina, of course not, how close I am to you and yet how little I appreciate your feelings. I should not have asked. Come here,' and she kneels up and pulls Dina to her, hugging her tightly. The tears flow.

'It seems so selfish,' Dina sobs, 'but I don't want my home and lovely children disrupted. I was an unwanted child in someone else's home when there was not enough love or money to go round. I won't create that in my home.' She stops crying and sniffs, taking Julia's proffered white lace handkerchief, an elegance she insists on however low funds are, and blows her nose. Then they both sit back. Darkness is beginning to fall outside the long windows. Above them there are bumps and squeals which may indicate an imminent invasion by suddenly bored children.

Julia stands up, smooths her skirts and lays a hand on Dina's shoulder.

'They really ought to go to school,' she says. 'When you can afford it. Don't move, stay by the fire and rest while you can. I'll slip out before anyone else comes and sees what an idiot I've been.'

'Stay.' Dina is her old cheerful self again, the wounds hidden, the childhood misery pushed aside, her dark eyes dried, only wet long lashes indicating her previous distress. 'What I can do is go through the clothes, you know how they go round the family as the children grow. We can alter underclothes and add to trousers and frocks, so at least I could help to make them decent, and they'd feel better. I'd like to do that.'

Julia departs, having fixed a time for a great sewing session and some music lessons for the boys. Outside the wind penetrates her thin clothes and she wraps her cloak tightly round her to keep warm, and thinks of Tom and Janey without one.

CHAPTER 6

Leaving London

The train puffs busily through the Essex countryside, beautiful despite the winter bareness, past mill streams and pretty Georgian houses, past grazing flocks and hovels full of wretched families every bit as poor and starving as their counterparts in the city. Julia and Edward, Tom and Janey, sit silently, Julia and Edward because they are hardly speaking anyway, Tom and Janey because they have never travelled on anything so fast before and are clinging on for dear life, staring in fear as fields, animals, woods and houses blur by. Occasionally Tom relaxes to lean out of the window and wonder how it all works, seeing steam, sooty specks and occasionally flashes of orange fire. Janey grabs his new, to him, jacket hard, fearful of harm that may come to him, fearful of her own predicament should it.

Edward, casually clad with a striped silk neckerchief brightening up his dark baggy trousers and Bohemian Jacquard jacket, adjusts his hat so that he too can see out of the window. Julia averts her eyes from his stunning profile. He likes Tom but cannot remember how he came to agree to bringing two unknown children from the London streets to spend a few days with his pleasant and generous family in the Essex countryside. His fine grey eyes narrow as he looks at Julia, her arm round the little girl, her ruched bonnet tugged by the wind from the open window; her eyes sparkle, and suddenly he remembers only too well the circumstances in which the plan was conceived. She is irresistible, and he can't stop loving her and her persuasive vivacity. Sighing, he turns to her; they might as well abandon their coolness now that the station is near; she was deeply offended when he attempted to change his mind about the journey.

At Braintree station a horse and cart is waiting. Edward knows the driver whose eyes widen at the sight of the two children. Julia he knows: she is a frequent and popular visitor, as was her brother Vincent before he died, and they both were transported from station to house frequently, courtesy of the Johnson family, for they frequently hadn't the fare. Suddenly, sunshine breaks through the thin cloud, and the whole operation takes on a more cheerful, possible air. Tom jumps up immediately into the cart, Janey, fearfully, allows Edward to lift her taut body in and then tucks herself in close to Julia, who had bounced quickly up, greeting the driver as a friend. Finally Edward loads the strangely assorted baggage - street children's possessions are few - and climbs up himself, sitting within touching distance of Julia, who extends a conciliatory hand, as well she might, as it is his family they are invading. But Lord! Her own family has always offered everything they have, albeit little, to friends, especially poets, in need, so why should not everyone else? She clasps his hand and her eyes thank him, and promise him mischief.

The house is graceful, half timbered, with tiled gables and gardens separating it from the farm; the children, silent already, almost bow their heads in awe. Julia attempts a smile with them to disperse the tension, but their eyes dart from each other to the shining curtained windows, the trustingly open white door with its lintel and brass knocker; no need to exclude anyone here, no charges to be made before admittance. Suddenly into Janey's frightened mind comes, from a distant past, not a house like this, but an atmosphere, where her mother would sit at an open door in the sun in the evening, sewing and waiting their father's return, affection in her smile. Until he did not return. She sees Julia smile and tries to return it, just a little smile, not with her eyes but with her lips to try to please this woman who she is beginning to like so much. Tom has persuaded her it is all right to go with her; he says it can't be worse than what they have on the streets. Julia, somehow sensing her thoughts, reflects on how easy it is to pick up two children from the streets and take them God knows where; Janey, with her fragile prettiness is a prime target for a brothel, boys like Tom valuable for work or the same. But not these two; not now.

As the horse clops and stops at the door and pricks its ears anticipating good treatment at this well-known destination, a small woman joins them and holds the horse's head for a moment, stroking its nose as she tells the carter to go inside for refreshment. He takes off his greasy cap in deference, disappears round the back of the house; she hands the reins to a startled Tom, who gulps but takes them.

'Fanny!' Edwards cries, and embraces her enthusiastically. 'Tom, this is my sister, Miss Fanny Johnson, and Fanny, this is Janey.' Do these children have no surnames, thinks Fanny. Apparently not.

Fanny's face is smooth, contented, burnished by greater contact with the sun and wind than her brother's. She is comely, rounded, at least a decade older than Edward; she looks straight at the children with steady eyes and smiles. There is no censure, no judgement. She trails a hand lightly along the horse's back, so that Tom is not overwhelmed by his responsibility, and moves to Julia, who warmly kisses her.

'So this is Janey?' The little girl is nearly invisible behind Julia's full skirts, light yellow wool, scavenged from some wealthy pupil's discarded wardrobe, not suited to the countryside but Julia's wardrobe remains distinctly metropolitan at all times. Julia brings Janey forward.

'Janey, this is Miss Johnson, Mr Johnson's sister. She's invited us to stay,' a euphemism here, 'so please try to talk to her. She's a very good friend of mine.'

'And I hope to be a good friend of yours too,' says Fanny, 'and your brother.' She gently takes the child's hand and is not rejected. 'We're going inside and your brother is going to take the horse round to the back with my brother,' Janey actually smiles weakly at the thought of them both being brothers, 'to give her some water and bran.' Janey falters as Tom prepares to disappear. 'He'll come to join us afterwards.'

Julia shivers in her thin clothes and Fanny propels

both of them inside with her arms round their shoulders. Her eyes say to Julia, 'I know what I'm doing,' as they pad down a flagged corridor towards a warm waft of air and the smell of baking. The farm's kitchen is cavernous and used for feeding workers and staff; the huge deal table has benches and chairs, and at the top of it Mrs Briggs, harassed, hair awry in the heat from the open range, and not completely sure what the missus is doing with the two children she has been warned about. But she greets Julia warmly, then wipes a tear with her apron.

'I've not seen you, Miss Julia, since your brother passed away! Poor Mr Vincent! Always my favourite.' Julia pretends to look hurt. 'Come now, you know what I mean,' and she wipes her whole shining face with her apron so that she can see better out of her sweat encrusted lashes. Janey stands mute and downcast.

Fanny looks at her and says, 'Mrs Briggs is going to give you some food before she feeds the men. Tom is coming in to eat with you when the horse is looked after. Miss Hunt and I have some housekeeping to do and we will be back in a short time.' Her careful phrases are reassuring but tears spring to Janey's eyes, although they do not spill over, for Tom enters, remarkably cheerful, and is told to sit beside her. Fanny pushes Julia gently out of the kitchen and towards a comfortable drawing room at the front of the house. She closes the door quietly behind them and they sit either side of a barely flickering fire.

'Now, my dear,' says Fanny companionably, poking the smouldering embers into a single tall flame and reaching for a log from the pile, 'let's try and sort this out. I—'

'I'm so sorry,' says Julia in a rush, 'I couldn't think of anyone else. I tried Dina and she really can't, she's got enough children of her own and—'

'Of course she has. I'm surprised you even asked.' Fanny has great respect for Leigh Hunt's family and their fabled generosity. 'But you asked Edward. Why?'

Julia took a deep breath and started the story where her cold hand had met Tom's equally cold probing fingers on the night of the Dickens' dinner. Fanny knew the Hunts so well that she was familiar with Julia's and Henry's night time habits; she fervently wished Edward would marry Julia soon and relieve Julia of her poverty and herself of the burden of the farm. She had other things she would prefer to do.

'I was into it so suddenly,' Julia is saying. 'I couldn't just ignore them. Although we do ignore children like this all the time and turn away from even giving them a penny.' She sounded fiery and was twisting her fingers together, strong fingers well-shaped for her music, now rubbing the wool of her yellow skirt nervously. 'That little girl - no mother, hungry, sleeping in doss houses which feed the brothels of the Haymarket, Tom full of anger that would drive him to do anything to protect her. I couldn't ignore them once I began to talk to them.'

'Did you think you'd be a mother to them?' asks Fanny quietly. 'Women without children often seek the children of others to love and cherish. I know. I do it all the time here. My brothers and sisters come to this clean air to have their babies and often return to London with their other children leaving the babies with me! And I love it,' she continued, 'all the privileges of parenthood without the permanent responsibilities!'

Julia gets up and walks to the bowed window and looks at the flat fields rolling away, flecked with freezing animals. She doesn't want to discuss maternal yearnings. Fanny continues.

'You don't need to be like me, a vicarious parent. You can marry Edward, bring up a brood of your own here and include waifs and strays! He can continue with his work some days in London - think how the railway has made this possible - and you would have me to help if you wanted me. And,' she added gently, 'you'd have security.' Julia turns from the window.

'I'm not ready to marry Edward - or anybody,' she says firmly. 'I love him. I love all of you, sometimes,' and she chuckles, 'I think I'm in love with the family as well as Edward. But I'm surrounded by women who have so many children that their bodies are wrecked and their minds distracted. I would like a child, perhaps one or two, but not ten like my mother! Not even five like Dina. And I would like a life of my own, my music, I want to learn still. Anyway,' she pulls herself up sharply, 'with real respect, Fanny, we were discussing the mess I'm in with these children and how you were going to help me!'

Fanny sighs amiably. It was no more than she expects of this talented, spirited woman whom she hopes one day to make her sister-in-law.

'Dear Julia,' she says, 'it's hard to help but here is a possibility. You stay here with the children for a few days to make them comfortable. They will have to be with the servants - the servants,' she repeated to stop

Julia interrupting, 'it won't work otherwise, it's not comfortable for them to sit with us in the dining room or here, and Mrs Briggs will be a far more familiar figure for them than you or me. Have you not thought about that?'

Julia had indeed given little thought to the practicalities of introducing two children whose time in the workhouse had removed any slight polish their hard working parents had managed to apply before disaster struck. Their deterioration on the streets since had further eaten into their manners, speech, eating habits and clothing. Of course Fanny was right. But Julia wanted Janey not to cry and Tom to smile; would this be possible if she was not with them? I'm not their mother, she thinks, quite savagely; why on earth am I thinking like this?

Fanny takes her upstairs to the room she usually occupies when she is staying, sometimes sharing with another Johnson nephew or niece, or even with her own, for Jacintha, youngest of Leigh Hunt's family and her brood were often here. 'I'm putting the children in the attic,' says Fanny. 'You'll hear if Janey cries, but she *will* be homesick even if she doesn't have a home. Children always are for a day or two.' Julia manages to stay silent in the face of Fanny's experience with many and various children. 'And after three days you must go back to London; we'll see how they settle and if we can fit them in somehow. It may not work, and what we do then I don't know. Neither do you, I suspect,' she says dryly.

Julia is suddenly hit by the enormity of what she has done. Two orphans, picked from the streets, transported to Essex, an alien environment with people they don't know; what did she think would happen next? How awful that it is so easy to do it. She catches her breath, steadies herself against the door frame, feels her heart thumping inside her neatly corseted bosom. What is Fanny saying now?

'That boy looks as if he could spend all day with horses. I'll see he's out most of the day. What about the girl?'

'I don't know,' says Julia lamely. 'While I'm here I'll try to find out where she likes to be. And thank you,' she adds meekly.

CHAPTER 7

Introducing Trelawny

Julia sits alone on the train back to back to London, rattling uncomfortably in third class; the hard benches hurt her spine and she braces herself to keep upright. The Johnsons have tactfully paid the carter to take her to the station, so she has been able to tip the man. Gratuities always worry her: caught between poverty and respectability, she frequently disappoints those who mistake her apparent sophistication for wealth. Edward had gone back the day after they arrived, washing his hands of the whole affair in a pleasantly firm way. It had shocked him that Julia had managed to bring the children, shocked him further that it was possible to do so; artist and Bohemian, he nevertheless respected the law but had imbibed from his engraving teacher, Linton, the basics of liberalism. To find there was no law to protect orphans, no records, nothing unless they were in the workhouse, enduring its harsh routines and separations, appalled and disturbed him. He knew that Julia's heart would rule her head as far as children were concerned. Would that it would do so for him.

As the Essex countryside races by - they must be doing at least thirty miles an hour - she forces herself to think about the last three days. Tom had, miraculously, seemed fatter and browner by the time she left. Although he still watched over his sister with the protective zeal of an animal over its young, he was capable of removing himself from her if there was a horse in sight. He swayed along on the back of the plough, jumping off and on to hold the horses' heads so that the Johnson's bailiff could adjust harness according to the heaviness of the soil. He produced nosebags and ran to fetch water from a stream when they had their break. On return he put on sweat rugs and made bran mash; he leaned upon their sweet warm flanks and breathed deeply their grassy smell. Eventually he was persuaded to return to the kitchen and eat the substantial evening meal served. His eyes widened at the sheer extravagance of it. At night they slept in the attic bedroom facing the stables, Tom straining to catch every soft blowing and whinny; he was even sure he could hear the horses' teeth tearing at the nets filled with hay. Each night they had been able to wash from a jug they had carried upstairs before going to bed and put on the clean night clothes Julia and Dina had reconstructed from the young Hunts outgrown garments. Tom eventually fell asleep, sheer weariness blurring the horse euphoria.

Janey had lain in her truckle bed, flat on her back, her arms folded across her chest as in death. She could hear Tom's regular deep breathing and her own shallow, short breaths. Her nightdress was better than any day dress she'd had for a long time; but even the pretty smocking at the collar failed to comfort her. She scarcely dared move in this clean bed, indeed in this great house. She felt she could get lost, and indeed had panicked when she found the back door into the kitchen, scratched and battered from the comings and goings of the farm and house servants: could this be the same house? The shining front door with its bright white paint and brass knocker had seemed to her like a gate to heaven on her arrival; she was distressed when she tried to re-enter the house from the stables at the back. Mrs Briggs had found her weeping on the stone step and briskly brought her in and sat her at the table with biscuits and milk. She didn't approve of this arrangement with the children, but she knew distress when she saw it. After that, Janey didn't let Julia out of her sight, and eventually fell asleep only because she could hear her singing in the drawing room downstairs after the servants had cleared the dinner. The next day they spent together in the gardens and the house, and the fugitive look began to disappear from her sad grey eyes. Julia's heart, normally within her controlled gift, reluctantly embraced Janey's.

Both children had rapidly remembered how to use a knife and fork; what a wash stand and jug were for; and finally how to say thank you to Fanny and Mrs Briggs, Tom a firm treble and his sister a whisper. But whatever next? She had left with tears from Janey, clinging like a limpet to her skirts as the carter arrived. Julia had realised at that moment more than any other the attachment the girl had to her, and her stomach churned.

Liverpool Street station is noisy with shrieking steam and shouting porters; she pushes her way

JULIA'S SHILLING

through the crowds, keeping her carpet bag close to her, smiling as she remembers her experience with Tom. The omnibus is packed but her bright face wins her a seat inside from a tall man who looks benignly at her. She smiles gratefully, sits down clutching her bag on her lap, a few wisps of dark hair escaping from her bonnet, aware that the journey will take well over an hour. She does not possess a watch, but the train timetable had told her that she would be back later than she was expected to be. Henry and Dina were on duty for her parents, and she becomes anxious that her late return will cause problems with their children. She sighs, closes her eyes, clutches her bag tighter. She's always chasing something, her parents' care, her pupils who live in different parts of London, Edward and his needs, her own performances in wealthy houses, even the lessons she can sometimes still afford at the Royal Academy. And always on the omnibus or on foot, trying to be on time. She recently lost a well-paying pupil because the omnibus to Richmond was delayed by a horse going lame; by the time she reached the house the young woman had gone to a social engagement and her mother told the maid who opened the door to tell Miss Hunt she need not call again. She jolts out of this self-indulgent reverie as she realises she must stop the bus and get off; the harness jingles in the darkness as the horses push forward and she is left alone at the roadside.

There are several lights burning in the houses in Cornwall Road; her father's and Henry's are next to each other. Tentatively she pushes the door of her father's and listens: has her late arrival created any problems? Henry emerges silently from the kitchen with a finger on his lips and a bowl in his other hand;

from the parlour there is a deep voiced laughter; together they mount the stairs to their mother's room.

'Who's in with Papa?' whispers Julia.

'Tre.'

'Lord above!'

'Don't tell Ma or she'll want him upstairs for hours and then he'll never leave and will have to stay the night.' Henry sighs. 'And we've got Claire next door and I cannot sit through hours and hours of when we wazzas.'

Julia giggles. 'The stories make me laugh,' she whispers, 'but only the first time I hear them.' They pause at Marianne's door. Julia goes first.

'Hello, dearest,' she says, fondly kissing the ruin of the once handsome woman propped up in the bed, a single candle burning at the bedside, an empty bottle beside it. 'I'm a bit late but Henry has your supper. Had a good day?' Marianne Hunt, alcoholic and arthritic, is no fool.

'Would you, here alone with no medicine left?' she replies tartly. Her ancient lace cap is tilted over one eye and her appearance is both tragic and comical. Henry leans over and straightens it. Both children stand back and survey their parent. She has borne ten children, lost one, cared for the others with passion, love and ingenuity, gathered a reputation for fecklessness as she struggled with debt and her husband's impoverishing principles. Now her comfort is brandy and rum, a loving but uncomprehending husband, and memories which are fading fast. Henry places the bowl of stew on a tray and encourages her to eat. She doesn't. Her gnarled hand reaches towards the empty bottle and she hands it to him, looking directly at him, silently. The both know when they are beaten and take the view that it's a reasonable compromise - her past loving care for them exchanged for her comfort now. They go downstairs, Julia having exacted a promise of a refilled bottle for two spoonsful of stew.

'Don't let Dina end up like that,' Julia says to Henry. 'Mary Shelley once told Ma that women were not a field to be employed continually for enlarging grain.'

Henry whistled softly.

'Did she now?' he breathes. 'Can't imagine Mrs S saying that now.' Visibly bracing themselves they push open the door of the parlour.

Every room in which Leigh Hunt worked, including the one in the Surrey Gaol years ago, became a bower of flowers, fruit, tumbling books, perilously perched busts of chipped poets, a carpet of discarded papers, the deteriorating piano and a fire which smouldered night and day. Today the room was small but little different. The fire draws out of the room the pungent odours of past food and present flowers, and this evening the deep scent of old tobacco fills the air. Leigh crouches by the fire, feeding it expertly with small logs and stones of coal; a kettle murmurs and spits; his white hair straggles down his shoulders on to the silk robe he clutches from time to time, at other times allowing it to fall open to reveal haphazard layers of garments from a different age.

Also from a different age is his visitor, sprawled mightily in the only sturdy chair in the room. His great height and pleasing shape deny his years, and his swarthy handsome face is framed in a greying beard accentuating the brilliant dark eyes above a finely hooked nose. The contrast with his host's slender frailty is extreme, although the two pairs of dark eyes flash in complicit harmony. This is Edward John Trelawny, survivor of the Pisan circle; he who sailed Lord Byron's boat, and was his *Corsair*, who loved Shelley and cremated his body on the beach at Lerici. A surprising addition to the household of poets gathered in Italy in the 1820s, he earned his place through kindness, physical strength and his delicately embroidered fantasies. Now he's in London promoting his book, *Recollections of the Last Days of Byron and Shelley*. It is proving very successful, his surprisingly elegant style matched by his fantastical memories. He may earn more than either of them from it. Who would have thought it?

Julia enters the room cautiously. She is named after this extraordinary adventurer, Julia Trelawny Hunt; her father was never able to reward his friends for kindness or loans, so he included them in his children's names, as a gift. Tre had offered Leigh money during one particularly desperate moment in the Hunt finances, but Leigh was unable to accept it because it was offered rather than requested. Tre's reward for his kindness was being Julia's namesake. As a child it had not inconvenienced her; Tre was usually abroad fighting with the Greeks, living in a cave with his child bride on Parnassus, or farming in Wales with his second family. But since she had grown to maturity and he had shed the second wife, his interest in her seemed greater.

JULIA'S SHILLING

And so he rises from his chair and envelops her; his strength is literally breathtaking, crushing, and he smells of tobacco and rare ointments and spices. The embrace is somewhat more than fatherly. He is very clean, bathing daily and berating those who don't; he wears no socks and his strong feet today are in sandals despite the cold. He despises underwear, not a problem with his daily baths. Julia waits for the embrace to subside and gently removes herself.

'Carissima Guilia!' Always the Italian greeting; from her father as well as from him. He stands back, filling the room, and surveys her small frame. 'You look beautiful! Tired perhaps?'

'I'm always busy, Tre,' she replies, twisting hands betraying her unease. 'There's a lot to do here and there's the children and my music...'

'She helps us so much,' interrupts Henry, now stretched precariously on a battered chaise longue which their mother claims had borne the fragile weight of Keats. He can see Julia is struggling to provide herself with reasons not to be available to spend time with their father's friend. It may be harder than they realise. 'She's such a help to Dina.'

'Dina!' roars the great man, the voice rumbling from the cavern of his chest, 'lovely daughter of incomparable mother! I was so delighted when I heard that you had married her, Henry. You were both adorable children, kissed by the Italian sun, reared in the house of great poets...' The fantasy continues and Henry remembers how Tre had contributed to the deaths of both Shelley and Byron, mishandling boats and doctors respectively. Leigh Hunt mused sometimes that Tre alone had changed the path of

English literature through his involvement with their deaths. No matter now. Trelawny is already launched upon memories of the loveliness of Mary Shelley, of Dina's mother Jane Williams and Claire Clairmont.

'Claire?' says Henry. 'You know she's next door with us?'

'I have always loved Claire,' declaims Trelawny seriously. 'I have tried to marry her, wretched independent woman. We will go and see her. Good night, dear friend.' He clasps the fragile Leigh Hunt to him.

'We can't,' says Henry firmly. 'The children are getting ready for bed, Dina is tired. Another time.' Disappointment shadows Tre's handsome face; he prepares to argue, but Leigh holds up a hand so thin the firelight shines through it.

'He's right, old friend. Another time. Henry will walk to the Broadway with you to find a cab.' He lays a hand on the adventurer's arm. 'So good to see you. Not many people come now. Not many left. Come again soon.' His dark eyes swim with unshed tears.

In the tiny hall Trelawny's shadow looms in the light of Julia's candle. Henry hovers protectively nearby. Trelawny clasps Julia to him.

'And you will come to sing to my guests at Pelham Crescent?' he booms. Quiet, now, thinks Julia, or Ma will hear and then we'll start all over again.

'I'll try', she whispers back. 'Let me know if you want me when you've made your plans...'

She knows Henry has returned as a cold wind sweeps through the house. He enters the kitchen and stands in his familiar pose, long legs akimbo, arms crossed. Sitting at the table, she looks very straight at him. 'What can I do? if I don't go I upset Pa, if I do go, Lord knows what he'll be up to. His mistresses, his wives, they're all gone now, and he can see a convenient place for me. Don't look so surprised! I can feel how he holds me! I'm the same age as the young woman he moved into his place in Wales and drove his wife out.'

Henry lights another candle and places it near his sister. He leans forward and pretends to scan her face, diligently searching for wrinkles and lines. 'I suppose it's possible,' he says slowly, 'that a man might still desire you.' She pushes him away, laughing. 'But you might do worse than be Trelawny's mistress.' At that a sharp slap lands on his left cheek.

'You are unbelievable!' Julia hisses, keeping her voice down from the parents silent in their nearby rooms. 'You of all people! You who know that I would rather die than be beholden to a man for sex! If I don't want to marry, why would I want to be someone's mistress?' Henry sighs; he thinks he probably meant it as a joke, but he possibly thought it could solve a few problems.

'Dear sis,' he says fondly, stroking her hair which has loosened in the great Trelawny grip, 'you're the most adorable, desirable and talented girl. But you won't be able to go dashing about forever as you do now. You've no dowry,' he put up his hands defensively fearing another slap, 'even if you wanted one to attract a husband. You can't earn enough to live on with your music, and Ma and Pa will die and this house will go. What then? Don't you really need a man? And we all like Edward,' he added persuasively.

Julia is silent. The candle flame flickers from her fast breathing. Tears sparkle on her lashes. It's the second time she's heard it. But she rallies.

'I don't know what the answer is,' she mutters faintly. 'You're right in what you say. It's all about money, and I want to live like the women I know who can have their independence through their inheritances. But I'll not give up. Not yet. 'She gets up and takes the simmering kettle off the little range, preparing a hot and very alcoholic toddy for her mother. 'There must be some way. Give me time. And thank you,' she adds affectionately. 'Shall we go out and sing tomorrow night?'

CHAPTER 8

Slamming the Door

Julia sits on the window seat in Edward's studio, the fading afternoon light making it difficult for her to decipher Fanny Johnson's handwriting. She has loosened her hair of its usual discipline; her head ached after her last pupil, a particularly talentless young woman who sings flat; the dark curls frame her tired but anxious face. Fanny has sent the letter to Julia at Edward's studio, as she is never sure where Julia is and suspects that a lot of her time is spent with Edward. This pleases her, irregular as it may be, for she loves them both and still hopes they will marry and take the burden of the farm from her, though Julia is hardly rural material. Julia peers at the thick cream paper and the regular, garlanded hand; she is anxious to know how the children are, and what Fanny wants to do.

Tom is happy, Fanny writes, very happy, from morning to night a willing slave to his new loves in the stables; no bale too heavy to lift, no horse too muddy to groom back to polished perfection, no water bucket too heavy to lug from the pump for them; she found him sitting astride one of them, very still in the loose box, and the bailiff's son is now teaching him to ride. He needs little teaching. He still keeps part of his mind on Janey, distressed when he hears her sobbing in the night, but the rest of his emotions are directly connected to the stables. Janey. Julia can see where Fanny has paused, lifted the pen while she thought, let it dry out and smudged the next word as she took on new ink. The down stroke on the J is heavy; she is still thinking before she forms the rest of the word.

Janey is quite different. She has been downcast and anxious since Julia left, unable to transfer her affections to Fanny, or Mrs Briggs, or even Sally the maid who is closer to her in age and a caring girl with siblings Janey's age. Janey is no trouble, Fanny insists; always obedient, willing to help in any way to pass the days, polite, a quick learner... but her sadness sits on her and the rest of the household like a black cloud. She keeps her tears for the night time, sobbing softly into her pillow for Tom's sake, waking early, Fanny suspects, to cry again before anyone is awake to hear her. Fanny is at a loss as to how to comfort her; she seems homesick without a home, yearning for a mother who died nearly a year ago, unable to find happiness in her surroundings as her brother does. It breaks Fanny's heart to see her so.

Julia braces herself against the window frame, feeling the cold air on her back. She turns the page knowing that there is a problem coming. Fanny is very happy for Tom to stay; she suggests he goes to the village school for some days or part days in the week, and hastily adds that she will pay for this; the rest of the time he can spend on the farm for his board and lodging, for the time being. *For the time being.* Why does Julia feel a weight in her heart? She always knew it would be a long job. One step at a time. Tom is safe for now.

But, continues Fanny, it is hard for Janey and the rest of the household to live with her distress; her sadness is overwhelming her and the rest of them. She thinks Janey should return to London to be with Julia, for whom she has such a strong affection. Could not a place, on similar terms to Tom's at the farm, be found for Janey in the Hunt household? The letter drops from Julia's fingers. Edward, half attentive to his engraving at the work bench, is watching her closely. She bends to pick it up, reseats herself and sighs.

The Johnsons have known the Hunts for nearly three generations, and Julia's generation has visited the farm frequently, often for health reasons, like her brother Vincent. Marriages have taken place within the circle and Essex has made a welcome retreat from the fogs and smoke of London. Fanny has never visited the Hunts in London; she assumes they live as she does, but in an urban setting. The painters and engravers in her family are well supported by their private incomes, small but regular, from the family trusts. She does not understand that those who live by the pen often die by it, as payment for articles and books is delayed or dries up. She sees no problem in absorbing this unhappy child into Julia's home. If only she knew.

Julia places the letter on Edward's workbench, silently. He reads quickly. He knows it is not possible to take a child into a house with an elderly alcoholic and a frail old man whose lifestyle is impoverished by the alcoholic's habits. Julia becomes tearful as she talks about Janey.

'It's like having a baby,' she sniffs, 'Dina says that you feel love towards a baby when you see it depends on you. I feel that for Janey.' Edward chooses his words carefully.

'Janey would be happy if you were with her,' he says, leading her to sit on the battered sofa. 'If you would marry me we could solve so many problems; Janey's, Fanny's, mine—'

'And mine?' He feels her go rigid under his encircling hands.

'You can't look after her without other people to help you,' he says gently, 'you'll have to compromise at some point, even for yourself, if not for her. You have no money except what you can earn, and that comes in irregularly; you'll need a man to look after you eventually when...' his voice tails off. She moves away from his warmth and sits a little apart. Her voice shakes, the tears flow but she speaks clearly.

'There has to be a way. I can't accept that the only way out is to exchange money for sexual favours, even in marriage.' Edward stiffens and drops his arms; he seems to droop beside her. 'If I apply that to you, dear one, it sounds awful, but it is in fact what women have to do. Women even marry awful men just to have children, because they have this longing...'

Edward throws his hands in the air and catapults across the room, unusual temper suddenly showing in his amiable face. He lands on an ancient captain's chair which swivels and nearly decants him back to the floor. Steadying himself he shouts, 'We've been here before! You are the most irritating woman I have ever met! Why can't you be like other women and exchange economic security for sexual duties?' He pauses, aware that Julia's dark skin has flushed deep red. 'I mean...' but she is picking up her bag and bonnet, staring at him as if he were a stranger, not a lover.

'Right,' she says, twisting her tattered umbrella into shape, 'right, now I know exactly where I am. And I assure you I will never, not for you, not for Fanny, not even for Janey, do what you so coarsely suggest. I'll find a way. Please get out of my way,' and she pushes past him towards the door, opening it with difficulty as he was obviously not going to help her, 'and don't come after me.' The rattle of the slammed door leaves him wincing.

CHAPTER 9

Soirée with Thornton

Julia and Henry are due to sing at their brother Thornton's house. The evenings are lighter now and a short walk will take them to the Phalanstery from their homes just off the Broadway in Hammersmith. The sun is still up and shines through the trees that line their way; occasional squirrels dart their lissom way between the branches; tiny animals scuttle in the hedges; this is a good part of London still, away from the smoke and fogs of the centre, the smells and noxious fumes of the Thames; houses still have large gardens and market gardens are many; cow keepers can let their animals graze, and central city dwellers prefer the milk from here rather than from closer to them where the animals live in dark sheds. Bell chimes shiver in the air: it is Sunday, the night that Thornton Hunt holds open house with cheese, beer, conversation and music.

Julia has her arm through Henry's and although logistically difficult owing to the great variation in their heights and strides, she can hear every word he says. They discuss the music for tonight and the possible audience. Not like the Dickens' friends; these people will be political activists, Chartists, reformers, writer and poets, but all music lovers and happy to put into a kitty to have Henry and Julia, with their family atheist, free loving credentials from the days of Byron and Shelley, to sing to them.

They have reached Thornton's house; a sprawling extended residence dating from many different decades, surrounded by a magnificent shaggy garden, just beginning to bloom, sending fragrances from hyacinths and bluebells, even some wild freesias. Julia stops at the gate to catch her breath; Henry looks hard at her, but she assures him it is only his great speed which renders her breathless. If she says so... The size of the house does not indicate Thornton's prosperity, rather the reverse. It houses twenty-three people, all of them, except three servants, related in some way. London rumour has always had it that they share wives as well as expenses and work, but who is ever to know the truth? And as far as the occupants of the Phalanstery are concerned, who cares?

But as Julia recovers her breath, consider the constitution of the household before you make a decision on morality. Leigh Hunt's oldest friend lives here, Arthur Gliddon, but it is his nephew, John, who is joint head of household with Hunt's oldest child, Thornton. Between them they have ten children, two wives, two aunts, a cousin, two sisters and an uncle. It hardly looks like a hot bed of sexual licence. Among the aunts, cousin and sisters are retired and active governesses, probably fighting with each other to educate the ten children and assist the wives with childcare. Quite a burden for the two earning men, Thornton, a journalist, and John, an emigration clerk, to bear, and John sometimes jokes in hard times that he could arrange to ship the lot of them off to Australia. But they all contribute what they can, and flourish in the company of old and young. Thornton's extra marital activities, are strictly that: he has four children by Agnes Lewes, the wife of his friend and colleague George Henry Lewes, but they live with her, and Thornton still loves his wife, who sometimes produces a baby at the same time as Agnes produces Thornton's latest.

Henry, humming part of a duet from *Così fan tutte*, thinks that Julia could do far worse than joining this happy household if she is so set against marriage, but he would never dare say it. Her commitment to an independent life despite her lack of money is not negotiable, and although she loves all the women here she has a real disdain for their dependency. They open the wooden gate and make their way through the bluebells and budding trees to the open door, where such a cacophony of voices meets them, old voices, children's, men's, women's - all coming from a large room at the side of the house, a sort of add-on dating from the days when it was a boarding school for young ladies. As they enter, a cheer goes up and scattered applause breaks out; Julia sweeps an ironic curtsey, and Henry a deep bow. The room is packed with regular Sunday visitors of the London literary and political cognoscenti; children scramble and play around the legs of the grand piano, and babies, resident and visiting, gurgle and squeal. Julia smiles delightedly; this is just the audience she loves, people who really care about music. Someone is tinkling on the piano and singing a song in French. A blonde young man, sitting on the floor, blows smoke rings from his cigar to entranced children. Pulling off her bonnet and gloves, she glances nonchalantly into the silver bowl standing on the piano. This is where the contributions for their performance are dropped, and it already looks well filled. Her deep red satin frock, the yoke well boned to enhance her bosom but eased by herself to allow for her breathing, warms her olive skin and make her black eyes glow.

The room has a pungent air of clean sweat, cheese and beer, cigars; Thornton emerges from the crowd and kisses his little sister. He is sixteen years older than Julia, he the first, she almost the last of Leigh Hunt's family. He is small, dark, almost ugly with his curly dark hair and swarthy face; not unlike his friend and co-libertine, George Henry Lewes, and both are very attractive to women. Thornton is a respected journalist and a generous man. He smiles broadly at Julia.

'Sweet girl,' he says taking her hand and leading her to the piano, 'you've arrived at just the right time. There's quite a heated debate going on and music will cool it.' She sits on the piano stool, handing her cloak and bonnet to a nearby beautiful child; she can't for the moment think to whom it belongs.

'Thornton, we're very hungry - anything left?' Thornton knows exactly how hungry people can be in his father's household and sometimes even in Henry's. He pushes his way to the back of the room and returns with two glasses of beer, hunks of cheese and bread baked by the aunts. Julia wrinkles her nose at the beer and sips delicately; the bread and cheese she makes short work of. Henry downs both.

Thornton's company this evening includes several Italian and French men and women, people displaced by recent political upheavals in Europe, glad to find the open hospitality of this cultured house, and a little relieved it is so different from the less free evenings they have spent with Thomas Carlyle in Chelsea. Carlyle welcomes Mazzini, the Italian leader, and his compatriots, but the Sage of Chelsea and his frustrated wife have not Thornton's gift of gregarious intelligence, which draws people to him, or his fertility which mixes old and young. The Carlyle house is bereft of children and somewhat silent. Here there's even the increasingly famous Francis Grundy, making a fortune out of surveying for the new railways, and acceptable here for his friendship with Branwell Brontë, railway clerk and brother of the famous novelists. Literary London loves gossip, and enjoys his. Thornton calls for quiet, the animated conversations die down, and he introduces his brother and sister to any who do not know them. The newcomers are expecting the usual offering from a girl who has dutifully learned her accomplishments, and settle down to listen to an undemanding performance. They are shaken awake when Julia plunges into Schumann, Chopin studies and Beethoven's *Waldstein* to start their performance. Singing will come later.

The room becomes very still and even the babies are quiet, sometimes beating the air with tiny fists; the older children, a few still under the piano, sit with their heads bowed, rapt. Adults of all ages close their eyes the better to concentrate on the music, and a great peace descends in the crowded room. Julia plays masterfully; she loves what she is doing and does it superbly. Her touch is wonderful, like her father's; he taught her first lessons and then went into more debt to get her better teachers. Nobody coughs, nobody moves. The last notes of the *Waldstein* hang in the air for a moment before the applause breaks out, mingled with shouts of '*Encore!*' and '*Bravissimo!*' Her face is flushed; she loves the applause, loves performance, loves the challenge of giving a near perfect performance. This, she feels, is what she was born to do, and must.

Sitting near the front is a small, good looking, middle-aged woman, dark hair starting to go grey, eyes so black you can hardly see the pupils. Her clothes are not English. She applauds enthusiastically, patting a stool beside her as she beckons to Julia. Julia rustles towards her and kisses her before perching on the stool.

'Claire! I didn't see you when I came in! How lovely!' Claire Claremont, of whom Edward Trelawney spoke so warmly, holds Julia's wrists to detain her. They have a lot in common, music, desire for independence, desire for men but not their fetters. At eighteen she seduced Byron and bore his child, regretting the ten minutes happiness for the rest of her life, and mourning forever the child who died aged five in Byron's care. But she is nothing if not good humoured, generous to a fault, and now spending time in London in the house she bought with twelve thousand pounds left to her by Shelley in his will. It took her twenty years to claim it as Shelley predeceased his father and the old man lived to be ninety. She pulls Julia down beside her.

'You play so well, dearest girl. Are you still stuck with grim unmusical pupils, or have you been able to give them up?'

'No, I can't. They're the bread and butter,' and she tells Claire of the relentless need to give lessons to support herself to do the music she loves so much. Claire is the right recipient for this tale: she has never married despite proposals from Trelawny and other men; until Shelley's money eased her path, she governessed all over Europe, learning Russian, Italian, any language required as she trekked from one country to another, educating her pupils to a high standard and earning their affection for her kindness. But marriage, never.

'You've managed, Claire. I'm going to do the same. You're a shining example!'

'Only just.' Claire smiles wryly, studying her hands, then looking up. 'I was getting very tired when Shelley's money saved me. Never knowing whether families would still need me, one of my pupils died and she had no sisters for me to teach... but now I can choose where to live, and how. Trelawny still proposes, he thinks he can re-create the life we had in Pisa with the poets. I just love to slam the door sometimes and choose whatever I want to do.' Julia leans forward and tells her quietly about Janey.

'Ah,' says Claire, 'the age old problem of the spinster, needing a child to love.' Julia blushes. 'We all do it, I have my niece with me most of time. But how will you look after her in London?' Suddenly she moves closer to Julia and starts to whisper. 'You could call in some favours here. Why should Thornton have all the fun of procreation? After all, once he has done the deed he has a houseful of women to look after his progeny. Your little girl could be happy here, you just up the road and ten other children to play with, all these childless women longing to care for and love her. They're all good people and she would soon settle.' Julia's eyes widen. She'd never thought of this house as a solution for Janey; even if it is not for her, she must think about it for Janey, if only for a short time. She squeezes Claire's hand as she sees Thornton coming towards her. The next part of the evening must start.

'Are you and Henry ready to sing?' he asks, resting a hand fondly on Claire's shoulder. When he was ten he knew her in Italy when she was in the throes of her passion for Byron. 'George wants to sing one of his naughty French songs and would like you to accompany him.'

'All right,' Julia says, eyeing Mr Lewes cautiously across the room, where he entertains the foreign visitors in his many fluent languages; she is wary of being sucked into some intrigue but surely his affair with George Eliot, as well as his still present wife, is enough for him, but you never know... 'Henry and I will sing first, and then I'll play for him.' They move back to the piano, treading carefully over the bodies of children, some now sleeping, and the room settles again into silence and anticipation. Henry introduces the arias, his charm would ensure a rapturous reception even if the performance was mediocre But it is not. They range through the usual Mozart arias, and then on to less familiar new Verdi. The Italians in the audience have tears in their eyes, and call for more over and over again, until even Henry is tired and Julia's voice sounds strained. At this point Mr Lewes comes to the front and leans upon the piano.

'You promised!' he says plaintively, 'beautiful Julia,

you promised to play for me!' There is a stirring in the audience, a few rumblings, a few 'Nos!', as clearly the majority would prefer to hear the Hunts rather than Lewes. But he is rescuing her. She needs to stop singing, and accompanying George's French songs will give her voice a rest. He hands her his music, and, glancing at it, she smiles. The rebels in the room settle down, defeated, and are surprised to find themselves liking Lewes's excellent baritone and perfect French. Julia revives, her eyes shine, and she falls in with Lewes with the skill of a born accompanist.

All done, she leaves the piano and returns to sit with Claire, as the audience regroups, smaller ones to bed, even smaller ones remain asleep in arms and propped on cushions on chairs; the men light new cigars and refill glasses, plates and glasses chink softly as the women move them round with the weary servants, who do not resent the long hours as this household treats them well. Claire and Julia huddle together.

'Just ask him, Julia,' Claire says. 'You could shame him into it really, although he's good hearted enough not to need it.' She remembers him in Italy, precocious, spoiled but intensely loving. 'He'll realise what a weak position he's in! Do it soon for your own sake as well as the child's.' And she turns to greet another old friend who is standing in a patient queue. 'Cara!'

Julia threads her way towards Thornton. She has to see him anyway as he will have the important silver bowl containing their fee, and Henry is too diffident to pursue it. The throng is lessening now and she soon has him in a corner near the table being cleared of any remaining food. He smiles at her and rattles the bowl playfully. She equally playfully responds by opening her carpet bag wide, and he pours the shining coins in to it.

'Well earned,' he says, kissing her on the cheek. 'I think you both get better and better. And the way you accompany old George! Marvellous!'

'Since you mention George,' she replies carefully, 'I have been thinking of you and him this evening, when not entertaining your guests.' He raises an eyebrow quizzically. 'Just your children, and his, and how well they get on together.' Thornton looks suspiciously at her. 'You have ten here, with the Gliddons, and then there are seven with Agnes... three, or is it four of which are yours...?'

'Julia, what's all this about? You're not usually one to congratulate a fellow on his offspring...'

'No I'm not. You know my views. But I wondered if you could help with a little problem I have?' He was about to laugh but she placed her hand firmly across his mouth. 'No, it's not that. Unlike you I am careful, as they say.' And then she tells him rapidly of Janey's plight. She can see his face softening as she expands the story; he has girls among his assorted children and is thinking of them in such a predicament. He takes his little sister in his arms and squeezes her shoulders.

'I'll talk to Kate. No,' he raises a hand, 'there's no need for you to contribute to her keep; use it for our parents, you save me time and money there.' He leaves her to bid his guests farewell. Julia sinks into a chair, exhausted, relieved and hopeful. So easy!

CHAPTER 10

Mrs Dickens Transplanted

Julia's carpet bag seems heavier than its contents; her mother had pressed upon her, dictatorially, from her rumpled bed, bramble jelly for Mrs Dickens, fruit thriftily gathered by Dina's children from the hedges at the bottom of their garden, transformed by Dina and her mother into a glistening jewel and distributed among the family; her father had added a slim volume of poetry. What the abandoned wife of the great novelist will make of these offerings Julia cannot anticipate. But she knows, as she trudges in the fierce summer heat, almost overpowered by the stink of the canal, that she needs to rest. The half-finished houses stand like old teeth, dust rising from them into the dry heat. Ahead of her is a solitary tree which has escaped the builders' clearances; a stump nearby provides a seat and she spreads her skirts in its shade; what bliss that her crinoline, a newly acquired cast-off from her most talented pupil, gives such airy relief in this torrid weather. The cage holds the skirt well away from her legs, and if there ever is a breeze, it circulates deliciously to her nether regions. She thinks gratefully of the giver, Sarah Baxter, talented, kind and wealthy; she puckers her forehead as she remembers Sarah's imminent departure for Paris and the conservatoire. No, she is not jealous; Julia's good nature has always overcome the unfairness of life, wealthy people with no talent, poor people with much; this girl will use her opportunity, until she marries and forgets her talent. But she will no longer be Julia's pupil, and Julia will miss the money.

The busy landscape shimmers; a skinny black dog with a grey muzzle and its tail between its legs hovers near and fixes her with sad brown eyes. She clicks her fingers for it to approach, reaching into the depths of her bag for the bread and cheese she had wrapped in a cloth before she began her walk; the dog becomes alert, moves hopefully towards her; her hand strokes its domed head and the soft muzzle urgently nuzzles her cupped hand for the bread. She persuades it to sit beside her in the shade; her family's finances have never allowed for the inclusion of pets, but she loves dogs and once heard their near neighbour in Chelsea, Jane Carlyle say, 'The more I see of men, the more I like dogs.' This is an elderly bitch; perhaps alone after the death of someone dear, or as homeless as the family who once owned her. She cradles her head in her lap, thinking of all the things people say about why you shouldn't - fleas, disease, rabies. The old dog sighs happily and closes her eyes. Julia will have to sit for a while longer.

All around her the frantic building work of north London continues; houses have been pulled down for the railways, poor people removed from their homes; she has passed shacks on her way here where families shelter with swarming children clad in rags, so thin you'd think their little limbs would break. She knew Shelley had wanted revolution, and that the French had killed their king until the streets of Paris ran with blood. But nothing seems to happen here. Stroking the dog's head she closes her eyes to shut out thoughts of the weak, the diseased, the dispossessed. It is all about money. Money feeds and clothes, educates, shelters, provides choice; but if you have none in your pocket you can't eat, buy or rent. Tin, as fashionable young men call it, or the lack of it, can bring you to luxury and pleasure or starvation and homelessness. She narrows her eyes against the sun and sees nearby a cluster of builders' labourers resting; these are not skilled carpenters and stonemasons, but itinerant men who work by the day and are laid off the moment their speculative masters can't pay them. Their lives are as precarious as the dog's. One of the younger ones waves to her; he is scantily clad for the heat, and his fine body contrasts with the older men, whose limbs are twisted from accidents, wasted and gnarled from disease and malnutrition. She carefully moves the dog's head from her lap, gets to her feet, brushes the grey dust off her bouncy skirt, and waves back. She knows well there is safety in numbers, and that many of these men will be good people fallen on hard times and labouring simply to eat. The dog struggles painfully to its feet and follows her.

"Ot ain't it, miss?' The young man says as she draws level. He looks at her appreciatively. His skin glistens with sweat, his muscles threaded and hard. 'You shouldn't be walking in this heat. Your dog?'

'No,' she says, laughing, keeping it light, 'not mine but she needs feeding. She wants to follow me now. I've a fair way to go and I can't really have her with me.'

'Give 'er 'ere,' says one of the older men, reaching out; he catches her deftly by the loose skin at the back of her neck and draws her gently to him, massaging her behind the ears; she leans contentedly against him.

'We'll keep 'er with us, miss. Where we live we often take in dogs. Makes up for not 'aving the wife and kids with us. Keeps us company.'

Julia laughs again. 'I'm sure your wife would be glad to know an old bitch can take her place so easily! Is Gloucester Crescent far? I thought I'd be there by now.' They were looking at her, puzzled; she was clearly a lady, but walking in this heat, carrying her own bag? Well-spoken but pleasant with them.

The man who had taken the dog continues, 'It's about 'alf a mile, straight ahead. I worked on those houses years back. They're good but not that big for what people want these days. You'll soon be there.' She smiles, gives the dog a final pat and makes a prima donna's curtsey. The cheers last until she is out of sight.

Julia reaches the end of Gloucester Crescent and takes a moment to tidy herself from the ravages of the heat and dust. She removes her straw bonnet, an old favourite showing its age around the edges, but cheerful with a new blue ribbon carefully added at the base of the crown and tying prettily beneath her chin. She smooths her dark hair and does her best to tuck in straggling strands, replaces the bonnet and dusts the lavender skirt which is now swaying in a welcome breeze. The slight rise in the road has made her breathless, but her chest has been so much better since the London temperature has risen to almost Mediterranean heights. She hits her top notes with ease and coughs infrequently. She tucks the bag close to her side and approaches Catherine Dickens' new house. It is a solid, middle-class, yellow brick, white stucco softening the windows and door. But not the grandeur from which she has been so humiliatingly ejected from at Tavistock House. There her children remain before Charles disposes of the house and removes them all to their country home at Gad's Hill. Julia firmly pulls the bell. It jangles within the house, dying away in a fading echo. Time passes.

A small dusty girl comes to the door, soot smudges on her elfin face; she can hardly be thirteen. She stares at Julia in the sunlight, as if trying to remember what she should say. Julia helps.

'Your mistress is Mrs Dickens?' A firm nod, at least that is clear. 'Will you see if she is at home to Miss Hunt?' The child nods, leaves the door ajar and Julia on the step, disappearing inside. The drying leaves of the trees lining the road rustle as she waits; a single bird cheeps thirstily. The girl is back.

'Please Miss, mistress is at 'ome. You can come in.' She pulls the door right back to show Julia she is welcome. The hallway is bare except for a new console table, its bowed legs still wrapped in a shop's brown paper. The door closes behind her on the heat of the day and she follows the child along a cool passage way to the drawing room. There sits Catherine Dickens, massive but smiling, on a bright new sofa.

'Julia! You are so good to come to see me! Did you

get a cab easily to bring you here? It's such a hot day,' and she sweeps a handkerchief across her damp forehead. Julia ignores the cab question and kisses her friend on her perspiring cheek. 'We're all at sixes and sevens here. Molly came with me from the kitchen at Tavistock House, and she's not used to being parlour maid and butler. She was the only one servant I was allowed to bring.' Her face crumples. 'I've managed to get a cook, and that's all. Charles always wanted to manage everything, and it was easier to let him, but now I find it hard to run the household.' Tears block her throat and she wipes her eyes. 'What did I do to deserve this?' And more tears flow unchecked.

Julia has learned in her short life that tears rarely solve anything. She hastens to the other end of the sofa and addresses practicalities, delving in her bag for the bramble jelly and the book of poems, which she places on a little table, wondering if perhaps the poems were not too pertinent a reminder of writers and literature; she tactfully moves the jelly to obliterate the poems.

'This is a pleasant house, is it not?' she hazards, stroking her friend's hands and looking directly into her sad eyes. 'I hope Mr Dickens has been generous with you?' Mrs Dickens stops weeping.

'That's not settled yet. It's so difficult. I was not allowed to bring furniture from the house, I have to buy if from the allowance he makes.' She looks around the room at the new items. 'There was no pleasure in getting them; perhaps I shall grow fond of them. They are sad replacements for things I have had around me for years. I suppose he wants me to forget; that's why I am not allowed to have the children. Only

Charley is with me,' and the tears start again. Her large frame shudders with grief. 'Charley would not leave me and because he is an adult his father could not make him. The younger ones I see when he allows them to come.' Julia pats her hand firmly, takes the crumpled handkerchief and wipes her face. At her touch Catherine smiles briefly. 'Thank you.'

Suddenly the bell jangles again through the house; a horse whinnies in the street; in the intensity of the moment neither woman has heard the arrival of a carriage and pair outside. Feet patter up from the basement and run along the hall. Catherine looks alarmed. Julia wonders if she lives in dread of her husband coming with more demands and restrictions. She goes to the window and sees a handsome carriage standing. She tells Mrs Dickens, who relaxes. She must know who it is. She nods to Molly, who has run panting up the stairs from the front door.

'Are you at 'ome...?' Catherine nods before she can finish. Julia watches as the groom returns to the carriage, speaks inside the open window and pulling down the steps hands out a finely dressed woman. Julia cannot see her face, but watches until the red silk of her dress disappears from the stone steps. Then she turns from the window to await the new visitor.

She is a tall, middle-aged woman redeemed from plainness by her beautiful eyes. 'This is Miss Julia Hunt,' she hears Catherine say. 'Julia, may I introduce Miss Coutts?' Julia understands immediately. This is the richest woman in England apart from the Queen, dedicated to philanthropy, unmarried, a contributor to Charles Dickens' famous Urania House, a home for fallen women. What can she be doing here, visiting his discarded wife in her new, sad humiliation?

'Miss Hunt,' she says, extending an expensively gloved hand and inclining her beautifully bonneted head. Her dress is mulberry taffeta and shot silk, exquisitely constructed but not a crinoline. 'A pleasure to meet you. Can you be the daughter of Leigh Hunt? I have so admired his writing. Is he still well?' She means is he still alive, thinks Julia. And she probably knows about the Skimpole incident and that I am Comedy.

'Yes,' she replies, slightly flustered before this great woman. 'He is well but frail. As is my mother,' she adds to make the situation plain. Miss Coutts sits beside Catherine on the sofa. Julia is unsure what to do. She makes a movement as if to depart. Miss Coutts, used to the instant response to great riches, shakes her head.

'Please do not leave on my account. I have told Catherine that she must keep up with all her old friends, and send them her card with her new address on it. It is perfectly possible to make a pleasant and interesting life without a man. Don't you think so, Miss Hunt?' she enquires, as if wanting Julia's support. Julia takes a chance, as the newcomer seems to be friendly.

'That is certainly *my* aim,' she replies, settling onto a plump low chair by the marble fireplace. 'I love singing and I play the piano, and dearly wish it was possible to pursue this as a.... career. People always urge marriage on me; I have... opportunities... but I want very much to perform and it seems to shock people.' She stops. Miss Coutts was looking at her hard.

'But dear Julia has a nice young suitor,' interrupts Catherine, moving hopefully towards a bell near the fireplace, to test her new household arrangements. 'I hope she will marry him soon!' Miss Coutts raises her eyebrows. It seems this is not what she wants to hear from the re-habilitated Catherine; she is learning too slowly.

'It seems Julia wants other things besides marriage,' she replies. 'And she may well be right, if she can afford to be. Now that you are on your own, Catherine, you might well consider that both Miss Hunt and I are enjoying our lives. You could wipe out Mr Dickens completely. He has given you children, who will eventually return to you when he comes to his senses, and stops acting like a lunatic; if you negotiate an adequate financial settlement you might well find life very pleasant. You have the advantages - children who love you, a house and money without the encumbrance of a man.'

Julia gives a silent cheer. What a goddess!

'It will take time,' she adds, seeing Catherine's doubtful expression, 'but with the support of your friends you will find a way. Won't she, Miss Hunt?' The tone of the question requires a swift and positive answer.

'Indeed!' Julia is confused at Miss Coutts's desire to obliterate Dickens; she had been such a supporter of his philanthropic projects. But she senses an independent and original mind. 'There is so much to learn, so many places to visit, Mrs Dickens now has opportunity and time.' It appeared to be the right answer; Miss Coutts had almost read her mind.

'Much as I have admired and supported your husband, my dear,' she says, turning to Catherine, 'I will not condone his treatment of you and his family. He seems to have gone mad; he has no sense of propriety or justice at the moment. Forget him and live well. We will help you.' Julia finds herself complicit. The door opens and a panting Molly is responding to the servants' bell. Catherine orders tea. Miss Coutts observes the child with a practised eye. When the door shuts behind her she says, 'Catherine, that child is far too young for what she is expected to do here. I will send you a good parlour maid who will train her. I know Charles was a great controller but you must manage your own house now, take responsibility and take care not to overwork the servants.' She stops as the door opens and Molly appears again, this time with the cook who has accepted her need of help, and made the exception of a lifetime by climbing the stairs from the kitchen bearing a tray.

As they gather near the tea tray, there is suddenly another clatter of hooves outside; drivers are heard exchanging pleasantries. This carriage has no footman. Julia, nearest to the window, observes a small, skinny dark man descend; his dark curls make a frill from beneath his hat. She gasps. His demeanour is very swift, proprietorial. The door opens fast, to his cane's loud, peremptory rat-a-tat. You would think he owned the place. Actually he does. It is Mr Dickens himself. He takes the stairs two at a time, a man in a hurry. Without announcement he flings open the door, a small tempest of self-importance.

'Catherine! I...' he stops. Three pairs of eyes confront him. He has assumed she would be alone, easy to manipulate; he'd be in and out in minutes. Catherine's hand goes to her heart, she starts to rise unsteadily but is pushed roughly back by Miss Coutts, who is out of her chair and towering over the little man.

'Charles! Behave yourself! Rushing in to a lady's drawing room unannounced! We were about to take tea.' She keeps a hand firmly on Catherine's shoulder. She looks at Julia, recalling the young woman's humiliation in the Skimpole incident, and reckons she has an ally. 'It is some time since I received your letter explaining your reasons for leaving your wife in these circumstances. I didn't believe a word of it; that is why I have not yet replied. I want very much to continue our work for the ex-prisoner girls, but you make it very difficult. Catherine, is he to stay to tea?' Catherine nods weakly. 'Then perhaps Miss Hunt will pour.'

Dickens, dumbfounded while Miss Coutts is speaking, is suddenly aware of Julia; usually he is vibrantly aware of himself in a room and much less so of other people, so she has gone unnoticed. Julia, now prettily bending over the tea tray in his abandoned wife's drawing room, is pouring tea and offering milk to the two other women. His heart plummets. She doesn't hesitate when it comes to his turn, fixing him with a bland, equal eye. He takes the cup, ignoring her without thanks. He will see this out. He puts his cane on the back of a chair and sits, uninvited, open coat displaying the trade mark embroidered waistcoat. I'd like a closer look at that, thinks Julia, the work is really beautiful, but she steps back quickly.

'If I am not to see my wife alone, then I am happy to speak in front of witnesses,' he says adversarially, the actor's voice suitably adjusted for the small space. 'I have offered you,' he nods towards Catherine, 'four hundred and fifty pounds a year. That is entirely adequate for a woman of your age living on her own. You have requested more.'

'Of course she has requested more.' Miss Coutts's voice is firm. 'She is not going to sit inside these rooms all day. She needs a carriage, even if it is kept at livery, as you have conveniently seen to it that she has no mews. She will need to call on her friends,' he fidgets in his chair, 'and yes, she will have friends to visit and some of them will be yours, loyal people appalled by your behaviour. She will need to travel. She will need another hundred and fifty pounds at least.' Julia, seated again, is enjoying this. Six hundred and fifty pounds and a house! Fifty would be riches to her. She leans forward expectantly, ready for the next blow from Miss Coutts.

'That's ridiculous!' Dickens is almost shouting. 'She has no need for travel or visiting! A carriage is out of the question! Don't give her ideas. She is in this situation because she has been a bad wife and mother. She is not in line for rewards!'

Julia snaps. 'She is in this situation because you have fallen in love with an actress and want to appear pure for public adoration! You didn't care about my family as long as their caricatures sold your books, and you don't care about her as long as your reputation is preserved!' Miss Coutts purrs.

'Charles, you'll be wise to give Catherine what she needs and not cavil about pennies.' Dickens winces. 'If, as Julia says, you want to preserve your reputation in order to be able to carry on with this girl,' an outraged grunt, 'a wife who is happy with her settlement, living comfortably, will work in your favour. Don't you agree?' She smiles benignly at him. Before he has time to answer, Catherine rises, mountainous, furious.

'I *am* here, you know,' she shouts, 'it's kind of you all to manage my life but I AM HERE!' She picks up a plate with fruit cake up on it and hurls it towards Dickens. The brightly painted plate spins through the air, shattering on the fireplace but losing its cargo just as it meets him; it settles on his shoulder, trailing currants and crumbs in the valleys and hills of his splendid waistcoat. He looks down at his stomach, frozen. 'I have,' continues the abandoned wife, slowly and deliberately, advancing on him, 'had enough of your decisions. I am going to be like Miss Coutts, so I need money, and like Julia, so I need to be able to do things, learn things, oh, I don't know,' she falters but regains momentum, 'go to places, so it's six hundred and fifty or I'll fight you in court for a divorce and then what of your precious reputation?' She is out of breath and sits down suddenly.

There is a stunned silence. Julia starts to pick up the pieces of the plate, her fingers scratching the carpet as she pursues the crumbs, face down to hide the smile she cannot suppress. Miss Coutts smoothes her dress and rustles contentedly. Dickens rises and fastidiously brushes cake from his coat. With as much dignity as he can muster he turns away from Catherine, shuddering slightly.

'Six hundred and fifty it is, then,' he mutters to Miss Coutts, ignoring his wife and Julia. 'I'll bid you good day.' He wrestles with the door and makes a very swift exit. Then a re-entrance. His hurry to invade brought his hat and cane in to the drawing room. He furiously retrieves them, coming back into a room where three women are laughing unrestrainedly. His colour rises. The downstairs door slams. There is a jingle of awakened harness in the street.

Miss Coutts has tears of laughter running down her cheeks. 'Oh Catherine, you're through it. You're going to do well!' Julia is exultant and feels as if her own family has just gained six hundred and fifty pounds. 'Wait until I tell them at home,' she chirrups, clapping her hands. 'He'll think twice before he vilifies his friends and family in print or otherwise!'

Half an hour later Mrs Dickens is looking forward to her new life in a prudently managed household. A parlour maid is to arrive the next day, and Julia is to return most of her way home in a carriage.

CHAPTER 11

In Confidence

Seated opposite Miss Coutts and enjoying the cool breeze created by the movement of the carriage, Julia, for one moment, thinks she understands why women exchange sex for money and an easy life. The leather upholstery is of the finest and the studded velvet doors with their tasselled window straps and little lace blinds above almost make her laugh. She can hardly believe that she is sitting opposite this legendary woman who has offered her a lift as if it were the most natural thing in the world. They pass the builders who can see plainly through the open windows of the carriage that it is their erstwhile conversationalist who has exchanged her dusty walk for one of the best carriages in town. They do not embarrass her by calling or whistling, but the young man stops his stone breaking, leans on his sledgehammer and gives her a very slow wink. Which she returns.

Miss Coutts is still chuckling at the flying cake and great novelist's discomfort. 'And I'm so glad that you are calling on Mrs Dickens,' she is saying, conveniently looking out of the other window, holding the hanging strap as the bad road jolts them about, 'she needs her friends and to learn to live alone. You, my dear, seem to have an excellent attitude and she is fond of you. She is lucky in many ways - yes the humiliation is awful and her friends have to learn to resist Charles's attempts to draw them away from her, but she has children which I will never have.' She stops, looks down at her lap and hazards, 'Or you, if you persist with your music. It is a pity that you have to make a choice. Perhaps one day women will be able to have children and a career.'

'I can't see that happening,' laughs Julia. 'It's almost against biology.'

'What do you plan for the future?' Julia sighs deeply.

'There are so many things. I want to learn to sing better. My best pupils go to the conservatoires in Europe, and I, their teacher, am tied to good but not brilliant teachers in London.'

'Why don't you go abroad?' Julia hesitates, not wishing to admit the poverty that is at the root of her problem to this rich woman.

'My parents are frail, as I said, and I am the only surviving unmarried child. My married brothers and sisters help them too, but they need me.'

'And who is this young man that Mrs Dickens wants you to marry?' Heavens above, she's direct, thinks Julia; we only met an hour ago. But Miss Coutts was expert at gathering the information she required.

'Edward - Edward Johnson. He's an artist and he has a family in the country in Essex who we have known for years. He wants me to give up my music, marry him and go and live with them and produce infants galore for him.'

'And what do you want?' The carriage jolts to a standstill before Julia can tactfully frame her reply. She can hear the coachman talking. He gets down from the box, leaving the reins with the groom. 'Madam...'

'What's the matter?'

'A cab horse has fallen. It's the heat, madam, and they're getting it up but it needs water—'

'Give them ours. Don't worry about the bucket. Just give it all to them. We shall soon be home.' Problem swiftly solved she returns to Julia. The horses pull away and the journey continues.

Julia says, 'I want to be in love with him, or someone, to sing and play, to be free to do whatever I want when I want, and have no one to tell me what to do.' Miss Coutts laughs. 'And I love children but don't want to bear them. My mother had ten, and has a good husband, but her health is wrecked. Mrs Dickens has ten and has been abandoned for a younger woman; even the late king gave Mrs Jordan ten children, then left her to die in poverty in France.' She pauses. 'But I have a little girl at the moment,' and she tells Miss Coutts about Janey. She listens intently.

'I know about such girls,' she says quietly. 'At my house in Stratton Street I can look down at night and there are children sitting on my doorstep at midnight; men come out of their clubs and take them and... some are about twelve years old, children themselves, and they have babies.' She shudders. 'You did well to save her.' She leans towards Julia, her knees coming closer than she intends with the swaying carriage pushing her forwards. 'I like you and would like to see you again. Will you call on me in Stratton Street? Perhaps you could sing one evening as well.' She pulls a card out of her beautifully embroidered pouched reticule. 'Here's the address.' She leans forward and bangs on the panel that separates her from her coachman. The carriage stops and he gets down again.

'Johnson, Miss Hunt needs a cab from here.' Julia groans as she has little money. She will have to dismiss it as soon as Miss Coutts is out of sight. 'Get one to take her home and give him this.' She passes a coin from her gloved hand. 'You'll need to get back to your parents,' she says. 'This is the quickest way. Goodbye, my dear, and don't forget to come and see me.' The groom is holding the door open and Julia descends with dignity and grace, turning to her benefactor.

'Thank you,' she says, 'this is so kind.' The coachman receives his rapping and the horses brace themselves, heave forward and clatter away. Julia wonders why she felt no embarrassment at the gift of the cab. What a woman!

She is home swiftly and comfortably, immediately seeking her father who is sheltering from the heat beside the open French windows. A tiny breeze flaps the flimsy curtain. Taking off her bonnet she collapses into a rickety chair and swings it alongside her to create a breeze. She tells Leigh about Miss Coutts and everything that has happened in the extraordinary afternoon; he chuckles.

'Well, well,' he says. 'Did you know she was in love with the Duke of Wellington?' Julia gasps in delight, thoroughly pleased that her new friend has experienced passion, and says so.

'She proposed to him but he declined because he was so old and thought he would ruin her life in his decline. But he did have a staircase built between his room and the room she stays in when visiting. So who knows?' And father and daughter laugh uproariously as he passes her a dish of cold black tea.

CHAPTER 12

Solutions

It is early morning and Janey is half asleep, lying with closed eyes in the narrow bed, trying to remember where she is. Against the pillow her curly blonde hair frames a face that Julia scarcely recognises these days. Images flit through, and she settles for the one which is seeping under the pinkness of her eyelids. The grey light is beginning to show in the slit between the two thin curtains. This house is ramshackle but she loves it, and the girls who are still asleep in the other beds. When Julia told her that she wanted her to move from Essex back to London without Tom she cried all night and now she feels ashamed that she made such a fuss. She has never had so much fun as she has now, in Thornton Hunt's house; sometimes she forgets Tom for a whole day, there are ten children living here, boys like Tom and girls her age; right from the day of her arrival, when she huddled against Julia and had to be prised from her to meet this new family, they had all been kind and wanted to play with her. No one wanted to steal her few possessions, like the street children did, no one fought her for food. They were only too happy to lend and give her clothes to increase her meagre store. The adults are rather strange and like to read and sing and teach the children. Mr Hunt, whom she is allowed to call Thornton, said she would have to have lessons with Miss Kent, his aunt, and some of the other ladies teach piano and painting. Julia - oh how she loves Julia! - when she comes, Julia lets them sing and she loves that. Julia said she has a good ear, whatever that means, and sometimes she says one of the boys, Edward, has a tin ear, which makes them all laugh.

Easing out of her bed she creeps to the wash stand and washes her hands and face, pulls on yesterday's clothes and leaves the other girls sleeping. Holding the banisters hard with both hands to lighten her tread she reaches the wide tiled hall and goes softly down a long corridor to the big room where all the parties and singing take place. In the early morning light the piano gleams softly in the corner. Gingerly she sits on the revolving stool as she has seen Julia sit, then reaches out and plays the simple tune she has learned from Kate, Thornton's wife. She has quickly been able to put two hands together, and recognise the notes on the sheet propped up in the piano. She plays the simple tune very softly because although this room is well away from the bedrooms, she does not want to wake the sleeping house. Her touch is light, her rhythm perfect. Then she takes a deep breath and very quietly sings a scale as she has heard Julia do. Then another. And another. She forgets about being quiet and sings the next louder, the pitch perfect, the shape beautiful. After five or six attempts she hears the door click and open. It is Julia.

'Dearest girl!' she says. 'What a lovely sound!' Janey blushes and says she is sorry to wake her; Julia says she hasn't as she hasn't been sleeping there anyway, has just hurried over from her parents' house as her mother is ill and she needs to tell Thornton, and her aunt, Bess Kent, her mother's sister. Julia is a little breathless and is glad to sit down. She asks Janey to sing again, and joins in with her, guiding the young voice through scales and arpeggios so that Janey is amazed at her own voice.

Julia says, 'You really like this, don't you?' Janey nods. She cannot express how happy she is to sing and play, but Julia understands.

'I was so lucky,' she says. 'My father plays the piano beautifully, although we only had a very old piano at home. He taught me when I was very young and I knew immediately that I wanted to play and sing above all else. Is that how you feel?' Janey nods.

'Sometimes when I am in bed the evening I hear you and the others playing and singing downstairs and it makes me cry because I can't do it and I want to so much!' Julia takes her by the shoulders and kisses the top of her head.

'Then we must make sure you can. I will teach you now, and we'll get others as soon as you are ready.' Not quite sure how, she thinks, but I'll do it somehow. 'I must go and find my brother now. You stay and practise until breakfast.'

Julia closes the door quietly and hastens towards the kitchen where she knows Thornton will be having an early breakfast before he starts his journey to the

City. He is never away from home at night, keeping his visits to Mrs Lewes for the late afternoons and early evenings, as is customary with men with mistresses. Julia pulls a face as she thinks of what married women put up with. Thornton is kind and honourable, would never treat his wife as Mr Dickens has treated Catherine. He almost keeps it in the family, as he and George Lewes work together on the same journal. But not for me, thinks Julia. I do not wish to be legally tied to a man who owns everything I have and who can even spend my money on other women. In the kitchen she finds her brother sitting reading a journal, having made his own coffee. He is neatly dressed, and although his clothes show signs of wear, well turned out.

'Julia!' he is surprised to see his sister so early, sensing something may be amiss. He gets up and kisses her lightly, pulling her towards the battered deal table and a more elegant mahogany chair. Things tend not to match in the Phalanstery.

'I had to come, old boy,' she says, sitting down and pouring coffee into the proffered cup. 'We've had such a night with Ma, had to send for Dr Thomas, he's the only one she and Father will trust, because he's been around forever.' She stops, takes a breath. 'He doesn't think it's good. She may not last very long, she's so weakened by her... pleasures.' They both laugh softly. 'Henry is with her now, but Dina expects the baby to come soon so it's a bit chaotic next door.' Thornton nods. He knows about the birth of babies, having caused many himself.

'I'll come back with you now,' he says, 'before I go to work.' At this moment Charlotte, who does most of the cooking for this large household, appears. She is not surprised to find them, and thinks it may be something to do with the Hunt parents. They are good children to the elderly couple, and she enjoys seeing the white haired old man when he calls in.

'And how is your mother?' she enquires after the usual greetings.

'Not good', says Thornton, 'we're going to her now.' Leaving messages for the rest of the household, they open the front door onto a blessedly cool morning.

***

Marianne Hunt is barely conscious. In the gloom Thomas Southwood Smith sits, holding her hand as a friend more than a doctor. He is really far too distinguished for a deathbed: his work for sanitary and factory reform has made him famous; now he is the recipient, like Leigh, of the honour of a state pension, which has rescued him from poverty. He does not approve of Marianne's recent life, but blesses her for the past and the care of his old friend, Leigh, and their many children he has helped into the world. He forgives her for naughtiness which left Leigh thinking he had prescribed a bottle of brandy a day. Tonight he sees a very different figure in the bed, a handsome young woman, frequently pregnant, always poor but generously housing Keats and Shelley when they were in need, sharing scarce food with all the writers Leigh gathered around him. Her older self's thin dry fingers twitch and scratch the threadbare counterpane. The single candle flutters from her stertorous breath. She is clutching at the sheets. The end must be near.

'Can you hear me, my dear?' he whispers gently. Downstairs a door closes, a welcome draught fills the humid room. Julia must be back. Leigh is downstairs, Henry has just departed. Two sets of footsteps are climbing the bare stairs. Julia and Thornton enter, and Marianne stirs very slightly. Does she know them? Southwood Smith stands back to let them get nearer. He embraces Julia, smiling a little, remembering her noisy birth. She sinks to her knees and takes her mother's hand. Thornton, her firstborn, takes the other. Her half open eyes are fixed on them, her mouth moves, but no words come. As if reassured by their presence, her head falls to one side. Silent moments pass.

'She's gone,' Southwood Smith whispers. He leaves Julia and Thornton and goes downstairs to tell Leigh, who has watched all night, but, as so often happens, misses the passing, as the dying choose the living's absence to slip away. Leigh puts his head in his hands and the white locks cover his face.

'Fifty years is quite a time,' he says softly. He looks up and Southwood Smith notices a smile starting. 'My wife was a generous woman devoid of illusions of prosperity.' He pauses, stands and then goes to sit by the ailing fire. 'You know better than most the way in which I put our little means to the causes of freedom. She never complained, not even in the worst storm of our adversity. Judge her not by her recent predicament.' He stirs, unseeingly, the little pot of porridge hanging from the hook above the struggling fire, his thin figure bent towards the ash streaked embers. Unobtrusively Southwood Smith leans towards the fuel bucket and feeds the fire with sticks and coal. He will not contradict his old friend; as he says, fifty years and ten children can only be judged by the participants. Julia enters, brushes her tears away on the back of her hand and takes the wooden spoon from her father's hand.

'Sit, my love,' she whispers, leading him to a chair and enclosing his thin frame in a gentle embrace, 'sit here and let me rub your hands.' She takes the old man's bloodless hands between hers and tries to chafe them to warmth, gently massaging them between her own strong ones. How often she has watched these hands on the piano, when he taught her, and when he played and sang in his own and friends' homes. He was so popular, particularly with women, who never, to her mother's satisfaction, got more than a mild flirtation from him, although Thornton's longer memory swore that he considered his sister-in-law, Bess, rather too warmly. But Thornton likes to excuse his own amours by citing others. Why is she thinking like this? She stops herself and concentrates on his hands, says to the doctor,

'It's a shock for my father. Will he be all right? What can I do to make sure he is?'

'Do exactly as you are, my dear, and keep him warm and let him rest, as much as he will.' Thornton enters, his usually mobile face still and white. 'And you, Thornton, can you arrange a funeral? I've left a certificate,' he adds indicating Leigh's crowded desk. Thornton sits on a small chair which is shedding its padding. He twists his hands, preferring to look at them and not the people in the room. His eyes are damp; his sigh is not steady.

JULIA'S SHILLING

'Yes, at Kensal Green, where my brother is.' He smiles wryly. 'It's very popular now. It seems ironic that we bury our family in a cemetery made fashionable by the brother of the late Prince Regent for whom our father was imprisoned.' Leigh looks up, his brow furrowed as he grapples with this concept. 'I was there in prison with you, Papa. It was the Duke of Sussex's need to avoid a royal burial after his two transgressions of the Royal Marriages Act that landed him with a tomb in Kensal Green.'

'Stop, Thornton,' says Julia, as an untidy girl enters, balancing a tray of tea unsteadily. 'Can't you stop being a journalist for one moment?' She takes the tray and sets it on a small table before the fire, and starts to pour, her hands shaking, the cups, unmatched, some without saucers, rattling under her trembling hands. 'Just get the funeral done, he's in no state to argue about things which happened forty years ago.' Thornton looks as if he is willing to discuss it but desists after a very strong look from his sister. The doctor pats Leigh's shoulder, bows to Julia, and draws Thornton into the tiny hall. Father and daughter are alone.

'Just you and me, now, *cara Guilia*,' the old man says sadly, 'just you and me, but we'll be all right together, won't we?'

She passes him the tea, cupping his hands with her own trembling ones. 'Of course we will, of course.' A chill clutches her heart as she settles him by the brightly burning fire.

CHAPTER 13

At Home with Trelawny

Julia had not intended to sing at Edward Trelawny's soirée on her own. The memory of the strength of his fierce embrace at her father's house had sent warning signals that remained with her, and she still smarted at Henry's suggestion that she could do worse than become the old man's mistress. What was it with men, that they, with inherited money and the freedom to pursue education and sexual adventures, never paused to imagine that women might like the same? Would they fight for changes in the law? Hardly. Would they modify their views on sexual behaviour? Rarely. In her study of the works of Mozart she had not failed to note the fidelity expected of the female characters and the freedom assigned to the males. Campaigning for women's rights to possess their own money, for keeping their children after divorce from abusive husbands, even to divorce their husbands, came mainly from women. Even her radical father had remarkably traditional views when it came

JULIA'S SHILLING

to the girls in his own family: Thornton's two families were tolerated and even loved, and his suspicions about the fragile heart of the charming Henry went without comment.

So it is with a thumping heart that she approaches Pelham Crescent on this rainy night. She is in a cab, paid for by Trelawny, without Henry, who has remained at home to do his fatherly duty with the new baby, or at least to amuse the older children, which he is good at. She could not excuse herself from the engagement because her father loves Tre and would have been saddened by such an action. In his newly widowed state he is fragile; she had thought of taking him as a chaperone but abandoned the idea as even with a cab it is beyond his physical capabilities; he rarely leaves home now and her sister Jacintha will sit with him.

The crescent is a fine curve of houses, white stucco and black railings, facing a garden not unlike the one in front of Dickens' house where she and Henry waited for their opportunity. Trelawny's book on his recollections of the poets Byron and Shelley, together with money from his farm in Usk, has funded this handsome temporary address; for a man whose addresses have included most of the grand cities of Europe, boats on the Mediterranean as well as a cave on Mount Parnassus with a child bride, it is appropriate and dignified. The third Mrs Trelawny is still in Usk, so Tre lives unfettered.

As the horse clops away into the rainy distance, Julia surveys the house; there is plenty of light from the first floor drawing room windows, each with its half balcony; there is a fine lantern hanging over the doorway which shines on the sweeping rain, and down in the area more light glows from what will be the kitchen and servant quarters. She mounts the steps and is admitted by a maid, into the black and white tiled hall, where stands Tre's housekeeper, Miss Taylor, age undefined. The status of this lady is sometimes suspected to be more than domestic, but Julia keeps an open mind and hopes, in her own interest, she satisfies Tre's ageing desires. She greets Julia courteously; she has been told to expect her and look to her needs before she sings. She introduces a dark, curly haired young man standing by the stairs as Mr William Rossetti. He has been asked to escort her to the drawing room when she is ready. Julia knows who he is: her father briefed her well before she left home. He is the brother of the poets Dante Gabriel and Christina Rossetti, and is writing a biography of Shelley, so is strongly attached to Tre, drinking in the recollections and trying to sift fact from fiction. Miss Taylor shows her in to a little chamber on the return of the staircase where she can leave her cloak and bag; she gestures discreetly to a small wash leather bag which contains the coins that are the fee for her performance. A red rose lies beside them. With a shiver Julia places this as far away as possible on the window sill, but carefully puts the coins in her hanging pocket and closes the door, aware that Rossetti is waiting for her outside. Tonight's cast-off frock is an old but very fine green shot silk stiff taffeta with a lace collar, chosen for its modest covering of her embonpoint. It is not a crinoline, as she finds them impossible to control from a piano stool, likely to balloon at the most inconvenient moments. Her hair shines and she wears a discreet gold chain near her throat, left to her by her mother, the only jewellery she had managed to keep in her battle with money and alcohol. Julia fingers it nervously, takes her music from her bag, and with her heart banging in her ears, opens the door, poised, smiling at Rossetti as if she had not a care in the world.

The young Rossetti offers her his arm and they climb the rest of the flight together. There is loud chatter within, a great cohort of Shelley and Byron enthusiasts and ancient surviving additions of the Pisan circle, gathered to hear its most famous survivor read passages from his book of *Recollections*; over it all a booming sonority. This is, of course, Trelawny. Julia catches her breath and wishes her father could have come: how he would have loved being in the centre of this extraordinary assemblage. The room is painted a bright blue and the ceiling a paler blue. Her father says Trelawny always does this to remind him of the sea, and to keep fresh in his mind his days on Lord Byron's boats, and sailing with Shelley and Edward Williams, Dina's father. Julia reflects briefly that he might do well to forget the Italian boats that both Shelley and Edwards drowned in. She watches fascinated as he rolls his sleeve back and reveals to the newest followers the scars on his arm where he thrust his hand into the fire when Shelley was cremated, and he pulled out the poet's heart. Fascinated because she has seen it before and marvels at his ability to tell it anew. The old man is enthroned on a massive chair near the windows; the dried heads of Greek pirates grin precariously from the mantelpiece; opposite him hang two portraits by the female artist Amelia Curran, of Mary Shelley, the poet's wife and Claire Clairmont, who, Julia is startled to see, is there, beneath her portrait, no doubt stage managed into the position by Trelawny for the occasion. An enchanted circle surrounds her, with much *'Cara'* and *'Carissima amica'* going on. How Tre managed to hold on to these portraits is not easy to divine. Mary Shelley is now dead and Shelley's reputation has been sanitised by his virtuous daughter-in-law, a rapacious collector of Shelleyana for her shrines. She will have nothing to do with Tre, whose knowledge of the poet does not suit her fantasies. William guides Julia to a seat near them, where she observes the rest of the relics of the Pisan circle, human and inanimate. Dina's mother, Jane Williams, is present, the centre of another adoring circle in a corner. Presumably she has had enough of Hunt babies and has left Dina and Henry to cope alone. Smoke from tobacco in pipes and cigars hangs heavy in the air; Julia fears for her throat and chest.

Suddenly there is a great roar as Tre spots Julia. He is a mountain of a man, but leaves his throne with youthful agility and ploughs through furniture and people to get to her.

'My dearest! *Siediti qui vicino a me*!' He turns to the assembled company, dragging her to sit beside him; chatter is suspended to listen. 'This is Miss Hunt, Miss Julia Trelawny Hunt,' (he pauses while they get the link) 'not yet born when we were in Italy with her famous father, who was with me when the fire burned these scars.' And he draws back the sleeve once again. 'But he named her after me and she has the fiery blood of Italy pulsing in her veins!' Julia attempts a look both puzzled and flattered, which raises a chuckle from some present. Claire looks as if Tre is going too far even for him. But at least Julia has for tonight shed her Skimpole shadow; these people care little for Dickens and his mid-century morality; they are the remnants of the Romantic age, and they link her to that. He returns to his throne, leading her behind him by the hand, his fist so tight that her knuckles are crushed together. Then he turns, envelops her in an iron embrace, and she holds her breath against the oriental smells and tobacco, her face crushed against the mixed tweed and silk of his eclectic clothing. Dear Lord, just let me sing and be gone. She throws Rossetti a pleading look, but he is trapped behind the circle surrounding Claire.

I must be kind, she thinks as she turns her back on the company, and leaning on the piano, riffles through her music. He is generous when it suits; he it was who broke the news of the men's deaths to the two widows after Shelley and Williams drowned. Dina can just remember him being there and the talk of money and horses and travel, which he assiduously attended to when all were shattered by grief. But he is sexually threatening. Why should I have to put up with this? She feels so unsettled by him that she decides to play first and not sing, lest her breathing betrays her anxiety. She takes a chance with Chopin, hoping that the comparatively new music will absorb Trelawny and his friends. She plays so well that soon the room falls silent and only the spitting of the fire, around which the older guests have gathered, can be heard faintly above the passion from the piano. She is very good tonight. Perceived danger adds a distinct edge to her playing. Finally she feels calm enough to stop and break before singing. She rises from the stool, bows to the enthusiastic audience, and makes quickly for the door which Rossetti is holding open for her. Rapidly she runs down the stairs to the sanctuary of her little Green Room. Miss Taylor has kindly left water and wine for her, and on the wash stand, warm water and towels. She scoops the water to her face and buries it in a towel, patting herself dry gently in order not to disturb the carefully coiled hair around her ears. Suddenly, the door clicks and Trelawny is there. He shuts the door softly behind him, standing massively against it. Her startled eyes rest on him, the towel still at her face; she is mute as a swan.

'No,' she eventually breathes, putting the towel down, 'no, please leave. I need to rest before singing.'

'Just a little kiss,' he whispers, advancing towards her, 'just one for an old but very loving friend—'

'No,' she repeats her voice rising, 'no, no no!' He reaches her and with a practised gesture envelops her and stops the protest with his mouth. It is horrible, wet lips on hers, tobacco, cheese, spices, beard, but his strength defeats her, all her squirming is in vain. One of his hands keeps her captive while the other raises her skirts and explores her, moving in closer. Bracing her left leg, she brings the right one up into the centre of his body. Whether he is in pain or not, he loses his balance and totters backwards, his head hitting the marble fireplace as he crashes to the floor. There is a trickle of blood. He has left a space between himself and the door, and she dives into it, seizing the handle, slamming it behind her and gaining the stairs. Rossetti is at the drawing room door, and sees her below him, hair flying, dress rumpled. He saw Trelawny go into the room and is quick to grasp the situation. He runs down to her and takes her hand, appalled, his face deeply troubled.

'I need to get tidy,' she gasps, 'I can't appear like this!' He pulls her into a little salon on the other side of the stairs, full of books and papers. She has no comb, nothing with her. With his kindly help, she gets her frock in to a more subdued state, and crosses to a wall where a candle sconce backed by a reflective mirror hangs. She can see the outline of her head and swiftly tidies her hair with practised fingers. But she's trembling; she needs time, she cannot sing with her heart pounding. Can Rossetti buy her time?

'I'll think of something,' he whispers, 'wait here.' He leaves and she hears his feet on the stairs, the last half flight to the drawing room. The chatter dies as he enters; the door is open and she can hear his voice, but not the words. There is a short burst of laughter, abruptly stopped as the door closes again. He is back in the room with her.

'What did you say?'

'I said you had spilt wine on your frock and needed a few minutes, that the recital would be all the more inspired for being from a wine soaked singer...' Despite herself, she chuckles.

'Thank you.' She looks up at him. His face shows real concern.

'What?'

'Forget it,' she whispers back. 'I've just got to get through this. I can't not sing as it will get back to my father and there will be questions.' She is breathing steadily now. He extends his arm, she grasps it firmly and together they take the stairs and enter the room.

'Mr Trelawny has asked me to introduce Miss Hunt's Italian songs, some of them learned by her brother when he was a child in Lord Byron's house.' The disciples sigh. Can it get any better? Julia starts to sing, hoping that Tre will stay out of the room. But no, after the fourth song he enters as if nothing has happened, the blood cleaned from his forehead, as if he had simply been on a domestic errand for his guests. He sits beside Dina's mother, and stares unblinkingly at Julia from beneath his shaggy brows. What is he seeing? Some fantasy from forty years ago?

The applause is rapturous, and the links will no doubt have increased the sales of *Recollections*. She does not begrudge him that; it is a good book, true or not, and she wishes any artist well. She picks up her music and speaks to Claire, leaning over her and whispering, 'I'm going to leave quite quickly. I'll see you soon.' Claire nods and clasps her hand.

She reaches the door, touches Rossetti lightly on the shoulder, muttering 'Shut the door after me, please,' which he does, and she flies towards the stairs, seizes her bag and cloak, sidesteps the trickle of blood on the stairs, and, ignoring Miss Taylor standing by the door in the hall, takes the next flight into the basement, through the kitchen, out of the back door, up the area steps and into the wet night. With the fee comfortably in her pocket she hails a slowly passing cab, and instructs him for Hatton Garden. Money solves problems. It is time to make it up with Edward.

CHAPTER 14

Plans

Julia stands on the steps of Miss Coutts' house in Stratton Street, Mayfair; the butler holds an umbrella over her as they wait for the carriage to be brought round from the mews. He shows great kindness and civility, as you would expect from a man treated with the respect Miss Coutts has for her servants; there is no disdain for Julia's carriage-less state, or her twice turned gown. He talks quietly about the rain and the state of the streets, and when the carriage arrives, conducts her to it under the shield of the umbrella and waits while the footman pulls the steps down for her. She smiles gratefully and settles back in the luxurious interior.

Julia has called on Miss Coutts as instructed. It has been sometime since the original invitation, owing to her mother's death, but she had enjoyed her encounter with this famous woman and felt the interest in her was genuine. She arrives in a wet and bedraggled state on an afternoon she had found was an 'At Home' day, and happily Miss Coutts is alone with her dog. Julia watches with some apprehension as a small pool of water gathers on the fine carpet from the hem of her somewhat frayed skirts. If Miss Coutts notices, she ignores it, summoning hot tea and toast. Allowing a decent interval for Julia's recovery, she says, in her direct way, 'I was sorry to hear about your mother. Does it mean you are able to pursue your ambitions more freely now?'

'Possibly. There is still my father to care for, but my sister Jacintha may move in to his house with her family.' She pauses, not sure that Miss Coutts will understand the perennial problem of the Hunts and their spouses, their rented hoses and their fluctuating incomes. Jacintha's husband Charles, to whom she had been introduced at the Johnson's house in Essex, had recently lost some of his reviewing work and times are hard. It suited them and her father to move in with him. It also means that the house will be full to overflowing and Julia will find it hard to squeeze in. 'I will be freer, although I should still help them.'

'Then why don't you plan a term at a conservatoire - Milan, Florence, Paris?' Miss Coutts says briskly. 'Come to some arrangement with your sister, so that on your return you do more and she has a little more freedom? You won't get what you want if you don't plan,' she finishes, quite tartly. Julia can feel the colour staining her face and neck.

'I... I can't make many plans at the moment,' she says softly, 'I need... I...' Miss Coutts stares at her hard, her forehead wrinkling in an effort to understand the lack of enthusiasm this young woman is displaying, when she had had her down as one of life's graspers. She bends down and picks up the little black spaniel who is lying across her feet; gathering it to her rather flat bosom, she leans back in her chair and addresses it directly.

'Julia won't get anywhere unless she tries harder, will she, Blossom?' The dog sinks its head into her neck in agreement. '*Carpe diem*, Blossom, mustn't she, seize the day!' Julia supposes she feels more comfortable admonishing her through the dog than directly. Suddenly there is a squeal as Miss Coutts drops the dog and sits bolt upright.

'My dear!' she breathes. 'I am so sorry. I who have so much of this world's goods and money sometimes forget that others do not. You can't afford it, can you? And you would never say!' You're right there, thinks Julia, as inexplicably tears gather in her eyes; if I won't marry for money I won't ask anyone else for it. She finds her handkerchief and scrubs roughly at her face; Blossom sidles up to her and lays a silky neck on her knee. She smiles through her tears and strokes the domed head.

'I'm sorry,' she said. 'I don't like tears in others and never in myself. It was just the… the… kindness in your voice. It means so much to me and I will get there somehow; but not just yet.'

'You will!' Miss Coutts' voice is strident; she rustles in her chair; was it indignation or excitement? 'You will, my dear girl.' Julia bridles slightly, unused to the forceful nature of the intervention. But Miss Coutts continues. 'If you're worried that I'm giving you money, then don't be. That's not how I operate. I have funds dedicated to projects - ask Mr Dickens,' she says mischievously. 'His Urania House project for girls who have been in prison was from my female fund. I have a male fund, a building fund, a museum fund and an education fund. I give grants where they are needed. You need to go somewhere to improve your music. You will come into the education fund. Look upon it as a scholarship. I won't give you everything you need; I'll grant you enough for the tuition and travelling; the rest you will have to find. Do you think you can?' Blossom sighs deeply in the silence that ensues, her little jowls quivering in the breath she exhales. Julia purses her lips, strokes the dog and thinks. Miss Coutts waits.

'I don't know what to say. It's so kind. I never thought such a thing could happen to me. May I have a day or two to see if I can find the rest? I just don't know at the moment! I have an older friend who has lived abroad and can advise me.' Miss Coutts was suddenly all bustle. She jumps from her chair and claps her hands, a signal usually for food or walks that Blossom misunderstands.

'That's better! Have as much time as you need, my offer stands.' She seems as excited as Julia is beginning to feel. Inordinately rich, without husband or children, to have a new project and to see her money working thrills her. Already her active brain is teeming with other possibilities to do with musical education and poor, talented young women. She rings the bell by the marble fireplace and before it is answered she draws Julia over to the full length sash window which on one side looks on to a garden, lovely even in the pouring rain, and on the other, the street overlooking the entrance to her grand house. Leaving her hand on

Julia's shoulder, she pulls the white muslin curtain slightly aside, and says,

'Look down there, to the left. That is where I see them, on the steps. The little girls, I mean, like your Janey. Just after the gaslights are lit they start to gather, the dusk hides them and they disappear if a carriage comes to my door, but they creep back later. The men come out of their clubs, walk this way on their way home and pick them up, put them in a cab and no doubt deposit them somewhere else when they have done with them. Do you know, I even know some of the men? I met one at dinner the other night in my cousin's house round the corner in Piccadilly; of course he had no idea that I could have seen him. And then they go home to their wives and give them the diseases these poor women and girls have.' She stops, her hand falling from Julia's shoulder. She has stunned Julia by her frankness. 'That is why you have done such a good thing with those two children. They are safe. And you deserve a small reward.' A footman enters and she orders a carriage to bring round from the mews for Julia.

'Of course you must be driven. It's sitting idle in the mews, why shouldn't you? Just tell Johnson where you want to go.' She accompanies Julia to the double doors, lightly pecks her on the cheek. 'Let me know when you find somewhere good to go, then we'll talk again.' Before Julia has finished her thanks, the footman is pulling the double doors towards each other and then precedes her down the sweep of impressive scarlet carpet, where yet another holds the inner door open. He passes her to the butler. I could get used to this, she thinks.

JULIA'S SHILLING

So there they are: butler and Julia Trelawny Hunt, on the steps which may later be host to little girl prostitutes, as the carriage rolls round from the back of the house and horses jingle to a halt. Horses make her think of Tom; the doorstep of Janey. They have a part in her life now. She's not free.

'Where may I take you, madam?'

'To twenty-six Osnaburgh Street, please.' And she thanks them both.

CHAPTER 15

Beyond her wildest dreams

Twenty-six Osnaburgh Street is Claire Clairmont's house; Julia can think of no one better with whom to discuss this piece of astonishing good luck. It is a pleasing, solid terraced house built about thirty years ago, four storeys, long graceful windows to the upstairs drawing room where Claire sits, when she's in, so she sees the carriage draw up. When they were built, these houses were close to Regent's Park with little in between; now they are pursued by the station at Euston with its consequent new buildings, and the once yellow brickwork is stained by smoke, the green spaces disappearing. Julia, used only to cabs, has started to clamber to open the door when the groom jumps down and good humouredly lowers the steps. From the road she gives Claire a sweeping, triumphant wave, laughing at her friend's astonishment. The coachman raises his whip in a horizontal salute and growls, 'Walk on'. She is soon inside and running up the stairs, bursting into the room where Claire sits, upright, colourful, worn, but captivating.

This is the woman who travelled with her stepsister Mary Godwin and the poet Shelley to Europe as it heaved with revolution and war. The girls were teenagers, Shelley scarcely older; Mary's pregnancies and Shelley's moods were her daily cares. When they met Byron back in England, she was one of hundreds of women to fall desperately in love with him; but she was - maybe, for who knows? - the only one to conceive and carry his child, outside wedlock, to a successful birth. Ten minutes of happiness followed by a lifetime of regret: Allegra, her daughter, being Byron's property, was kept from her and died aged five in an Italian convent surrounded by marshes, damp and mosquitoes while under his care. Her hatred of him has lasted her lifetime, as has her grief for the child. She has survived by keeping it separate alongside living a generous and intelligent life; and Shelley, who loved both Claire and Byron, left her twelve thousand pounds in his will, as he knew Byron wouldn't. When it finally arrived in the 1840s after his father's death, she bought this house, moving from Paris with her fragile but beautiful French furniture, and took up with her old friends again. Julia has been her frequent visitor and, with Dina, a substitute daughter. Claire holds out two brown hands: her skin has become darker over the years as she has moved from one hot summer to another in France, Russia, Italy; walking and swimming has kept her out of doors, and in the sun.

'Dearest Julia! A lovely surprise, just when I was thinking I had a dull evening ahead of me. And the carriage?' Julia explains quickly, not only the carriage but the offer Miss Coutts has made. Claire's black eyes glitter with excitement. Julia becomes hesitant. She settles in her favourite chair, intricately carved in the French style, the back shaped like a shield, clad in faded silk.

'I would love to go to Italy, I feel I know it because of all the stories I've heard from Papa, but I can't just go and leave Janey now that she is so settled at Thornton's and enjoying her music. Tom is fine: Fanny Johnson finds him useful on the farm, he has her visiting nephews and nieces for company, and he goes to school. He's very happy. But Janey could easily be upset if I disappear...' Claire was familiar with the responsibilities of substitute mothers; her oldest niece Paulina lives with her, and goes wherever she goes.

'Even if she pays for me to get to Italy and a conservatoire, I still have to find board and lodging. I couldn't rely on picking up pupils.' She sighs, staring at the setting sun reflected in the panes of the long window. It had seemed so exciting, such good fortune; but she has responsibilities. Freed from her mother, she has gained Janey. Suddenly, the sun is gone, the room dark. Claire is talking, as if to herself; moving around, lighting candles.

'When Shelley died I had nothing, no one. Tre wasn't proposing then, he'd gone to Greece with Byron and married his twelve year old. I spent the next twenty years in Russia, France and Italy. I learned the languages, endured the pupils - some I loved and some were less than compatible - and at times I thought I would be destitute. I had offers from men, but I would never trust a man after Byron, and I would never trade favours for my dinner... Julia, this house has been less attractive to me for the past year or so. The air is dirty, it's noisy, I have to walk through dust and building works to reach the Park - when I came here it was tranquil and green all the way.' Julia starts to listen attentively but can't quite follow. She feels sad; she has glimpsed such views and is now returned to the foothills. But she's been here before; so she will survive. Claire is still speaking.

'Julia, are you listening to me? Come away from the window - I can't see your face. This opportunity is too good to miss. Tell Miss Coutts that you have a friend who is moving to Florence, who will give you board and lodging. I need the sun again, I'm tired of London and I love Florence.' Claire prowls the room, touching the backs of chairs, appraising furniture as if assessing its necessity for a move to Italy. 'This is so exciting - I just needed a reason to do it!' Julia is familiar with Claire's enthusiasms; she also knows she is unstoppable. Money and business mean nothing to her; her generosity with her new inheritance is legendary, her business failures notorious. She had invested four thousand pounds of her Shelley inheritance in a box to let out at the old opera house in the Haymarket, which disappeared when the new Covent Garden opened. She funds her brother who is ill, overworked and has many children; frequently she funds Dina, whom she loves, and Henry, whose weaknesses outweigh her memory of him as a charming little boy in Italy. Her heart always rules her head, and she has never learned to curb it since her disaster with Byron. But Julia cannot believe it is that simple.

'You can't do that for me, Claire,' she starts hesitantly, 'and besides, there are so many other things

JULIA'S SHILLING

to consider.'

'What? What? We just need to get to Florence, it's so cheap to live in the sun, there's no building there, no trains eating up the landscape...' Julia has to explain other things.

'When I fled from Tre's house that night... I told you... because he... tried to force me, I went to Edward. I felt in danger. It was the nearest I got to giving in to marriage; I felt threatened, and I was so frightened that I couldn't see how I could survive without the protection of a man. Edward took me in that night and now he expects me to marry him. How can I possibly?'

'You just do,' says Claire, flatly. 'Edward is besotted with you; I've seen it when you are together; let him think you will come back and marry him - you might! But learn this about being protected by a man: they often create more problems than they solve. You have to take this opportunity and I want to go to Florence.'

'But you didn't an hour ago!'

'But I do now! Come on Julia - be your father's daughter! When Shelley and Byron asked him to join them in Italy, he didn't hesitate, he took a whole family into the unknown, across perilous seas! You'll be with me, and I know how to travel and set up, I speak the languages.' She removed her scarlet shawl, shook it hard and twirled it back to settle on her shoulders again. 'The first thing we need is a contact at the conservatoire.'

'But Janey?'

'She can come with us. You say she's musical - I

haven't spent my life governessing across Europe not to be able to look after a ten year old. We can teach her piano and singing between us, and there will be other teachers if she's particularly talented. If she stays here she'll become part of Thornton's household, along with all the other kind, boring women,' Julia frowned at her, 'and probably a governess; if she comes with us she'll learn another language and better music, and even if she ends up governessing, she'll have better accomplishments. As well as sunshine.' She stared hard at Julia. 'There really isn't a problem, is there? Go back to Miss Coutts, accept her offer, talk to Janey and Thornton. I'll deal with the house and everything else.' She stood in the middle of the darkening drawing room, hands on hips, her eyes shining. 'And I thought it was going to be a dreary day!'

Julia's return to Hammersmith was on the omnibus, but it could have been Phaeton driving her in his chariot of the sun.

CHAPTER 16

Firenze

Janey stands at the half balcony, hands on the rail, breathing the warm air, listening to the boom of the great bell of the Duomo and the smaller churches' clangour dropping into its great ripples. She is used to the smells of London, damp, foul and foggy in winter, an overpowering stench in summer as she and Tom sheltered under bridges and in dirty lodging houses; but these smells are drier, earthier, more animal, cooking smells drifting out of open windows, smells she has never known but likes. She turns back into the room. The apartment Miss Claremont has taken is now her home, and Janey loves coming in from the street through the huge door that you can get a carriage through, sudden darkness as it clangs behind her, coolness after the light and noise of the street; then climbing the marble stairs flight after curving flight to their door on the third floor. The heavy door leads into a tiny vestibule, on the right is a strip of kitchen where Maria, their maid, chops and bangs and sings; on into a reception room and three more rooms which they all share in a configuration of bedrooms. Janey shares with Julia, and wakes early as she used to in Thornton's house and the house in Essex, but now there is no fear, no apprehension; she often thinks of Tom, happy on the farm, and she is glad that he does not have to look after her now. She lies contentedly on her back and gazes at the wooden ceiling, every section painted in bright colours with birds and flowers and here and there a coat of arms. How wonderful that anyone would take so much trouble to make a ceiling beautiful; so many beautiful things in Italy, the buildings, the paintings and statues everywhere, and the music. Although Julia is not religious, she takes Janey into churches and they sit until their spines shiver with the shining, piercing clarity of the music. Oh, to sing like that.

Janey turns back into the salon; everyone is out except Maria, so Janey takes a moment to tidy Julia's music. Julia is not the tidiest of people, but Janey, after her recent disordered life, gets real pleasure from order; she separates the scores on the piano into voice and piano pieces, tapping their edges neatly into box shapes. They are scattered over the ancient but serviceable piano Miss Claremont brought from England; most of that frail cargo survived its journey by sea; Janey smiles as she thinks that if these delicate French tables and chairs with their faded silk could talk, they might sigh about the journeys they have made with Claire, about the sea water that had splashed them and rutted roads that have broken their fragile legs. Janey had enjoyed the journey, never sea sick, just like Julia, and sitting close to the coach windows, like Julia too, to see everything as the landscape changed after their brief stay in Paris. And then the days here, waiting for the furniture, employing Maria, who lives somewhere in the bowels of the building with her husband Alberto, finding out how to bring water into the apartment. Miss Claremont could do everything, whatever language a person spoke, she could speak it or at least make them understand. She had friends here who she had not seen for years, and who seemed very glad that she was back. There were English people, French, Russians, all seemed drawn to this historic city crouching on the banks of the Arno, in a bowl of blue hills, pink roofs and rough, dark red brick.

Julia goes out every day to the conservatoire; it is an old *palazzo* on the other side of the river, and Janey watches her as she steps out from beneath the windows, out of the great door, clutching her carpet bag in one hand, now full of music and notes, and twirling her new parasol in the other, keen to shield her face from the sun in case she becomes as dark as Claire. Janey can hear her cries of '*Buon giorno!*' as she moves along the street and disappears out of sight. Janey is beginning to say things like '*Buon giorno*' and also '*Grazie*' and '*Prego*' under the tutelage of Maria; she enjoys helping her in the kitchen and learning the names of all the vegetables they buy together. Miss Claremont says Julia is not to do cooking and cleaning but to spend all her time on music - that is what she is here for. There is also Miss Claremont's niece, Paulina, to help with the apartment; sometimes Janey thinks she doesn't like Julia as much as Miss Claremont does, but who cares? Claire calls them all her family, and they must get on with each other; Janey wants to be part of a family so will try her hardest to fit in. She has met other girls in Florence who are living with distant relatives they hardly know, because their parents have died. They all know they must fit in. Girls need the protection of families. It is not hard for Janey; she didn't realise she had so much strength until she met Julia. And Miss Claremont? She has no men to protect her, or a family, so she makes her own. She wants to be like these two women, Julia whom she loves, and Miss Clairmont, her benefactor. In the kitchen Maria hands her an apple to slice. '*La mela*,' she says clearly. Janey repeats it. Then the word for the knife, and to cut. It's very easy really.

***

Julia turns left after the Ponte Vecchio; she is not tempted by the jewellers populating the bridge, although she delights in their craft, because she has no money, and is, as ever, a realist. She can hardly believe she is under these blue skies, bluer than she has ever seen; that she has an apartment to go back to, a conservatoire where she is a welcome student, simply by handing over Miss Coutts's money, changed into florins. She has a teacher for singing, and another for the piano; she has some elegant muslin frocks in pastel colours, run up from old bolts of material found in their mother's room by Jacintha when she moved into the house with her family. Grateful for a solution to their crisis, Jacintha was happy to speed Julia on her way to Florence, and her skill with a needle is the best in the family. Julia flicks her pretty, billowing skirt behind her, away from a dusty hollow, and raising her parasol, for a moment, faces the blessed sun. She has everything she wants; jewels would be superfluous. Miss Coutts's money and Claire's impulsive nature have taken care of her. If there is a God, which she very much doubts, she would thank him. And it is so good to be away from London.

Leaving Edward had been difficult, not because she would miss him - she possibly might - but because the night she had gone to him after the Trelawny recital had been an unspoken admittance that she needed protecting. Attached to Edward she was less likely to be preyed upon; but he had assumed she wanted the protection of marriage, which he longed for, because, quite simply, he loved her. Miss Coutts' offer came just in time for her to plead opportunity and send Edward into paroxysms of frustration: there had been a stormy scene in the studio where their lovemaking had tumbled over into furious rage which had left the mice scuttling for cover. But this time she had not stormed out; she had been tender and soothing, and rather dishonest, as she assured him she would be back and all would be well.

As she walks along the Via Tuornabuoni, she reflects that here the beggars are at least warm, even at night, under starry skies. But Janey needs any spare money Julia has, and it must go towards her education, particularly her musical education. Julia crosses parasol with bag and hugs herself with sheer pleasure at the thought of Janey's love of music; all the musicians she knew, as well as her favourite composers, had music in their backgrounds; she had played the piano with her father and sang with Henry all her life; what a chance that Janey, orphaned, on the streets, in the workhouse, had this music from some distant inheritance so strong that it lay dormant until awoken by the circumstances of the Hunts' soirées?

And then her progress, so quick, so instinctive! Claire and Julia watched her little hands on the keyboard, watched her unwavering eye as she connected note and hands, had only to say once, 'Imagine you are holding an egg in your hand' for her to keep a strong and beautiful shape. Who knows what her journey in music will be?

Julia runs lightly up the steps of the conservatoire, an ancient *palazzo*, given by a wealthy aristocrat in memory of his musical dead daughter, carried off at seventeen by the cholera in Lucca. Every year a concert takes place where the students entertain her stricken parents with suitably mournful music in the ball room which has become the concert hall. Julia is waiting to hear what she is to sing: she hopes it is Dido's lament from *Dido and Aeneas*, which Professore Righi has been working on with her; he calls her his 'English nightingale' from the English nest of singing birds, and feels an English composer is right for her. She clicks her parasol down and glides softly across the grey marble floor, her frock swishing in the silence. Suddenly, it is broken; a distant soprano bursts into a Verdi aria, accompanied by a tired *répétiteur*; Julia winces; she is slightly off key. She climbs several more beautiful flights of marble stairs before she arrives at the Professore's room. The double mahogany doors, framed in curved ormolu, are shut. She knocks gently; no answer; another knock; she enters quietly, not wanting to wake the sleeper.

He is lying on a day bed beneath the open window, a breeze blowing the muslin curtains, one of which has become draped across his chest. He is a stocky man, not short but not tall in the English breed; his black hair is curly and dense, threaded with grey, and his swarthy skin betrays a man well into middle age. In sleep his face has a tired beauty; the usually strong lines from nose to mouth are softened and the frown between his eyes almost disappears. She sits at the piano and gets her ear in with a chord of G minor and then starts to sing the *Lament* softly to herself. A few bars bring him swiftly across the room and she makes room for him on the stool. He takes over the accompaniment, square, efficient hands transposing it to see if she can go into a higher register. Then stops.

'*Guilia, mia cara*, that is better. This book has it as a mezzo. You are not.' He smiles at her, wide mouth, good teeth, only two missing. 'Now, breathe. Breathe.' He stands up, gets behind her, places his hands on her corsetless ribs, easily found beneath their gauzy covering. 'More breath. Better. In. Out. Remember that singing is with the mind *and* the body.' Her voice soars, helped a little by the magnificently high painted ceiling, but mainly it is her. 'Push me away, push harder, harder.' When she first came to him she was anxious that his insistent physical contact would lead to dangerous intimacies, which when refused would ruin her lessons with the best voice teacher in Florence. But he has never been anything but professional; his passion is for their art, together, how he can make her achieve her potential. He has eight children, from babies to young women, and works all day and most of the evenings to keep them fed and clothed and sheltered. He reminds her of her father. There is a civility in Italian men which she values.

After an hour she is singing magnificently and it is decided that she will sing the *Lament* for the concert, a week away; he asks if she is to play the piano as well, and will she play for him the piece her piano teacher has chosen? He perches on the end of the day bed, eyes narrowed, his loose white shirt trapped in his folded arms. She plays two movements from Beethoven sonatas, passionately, accurately, as if her life depended on it. He turns to the window, so she does not see the tears glisten.

CHAPTER 17

Letters from Home

Janey and Maria have spent most of the morning sponging and ironing Julia's green silk frock; here is a beer stain gathered at Thornton's soirée when an enthusiastic young man bent too close; on the hem some darkening from a muddy London walk; and finally a tear where she caught it in the back door as she fled Trelawny's house. Janey was taught to sew by her dead mother; Maria knows all about laundry and ancient methods of cleaning beautiful materials. Now they have finished and it hangs, restored, on the back of the salon door, awaiting her arrival from a piano lesson at the conservatoire. Claire is out, calling on friends. Paulina, her niece, is in the salon having an Italian lesson.

Maria prepares a cool lemonade for them and leaves some for Julia and Paulina. The sun filters in through the half closed shutters, catching Janey's blonde curls; she has a classic English look which the Italians love, pink skin and blue eyes. She is nearly unrecognisable from the grimy, thin child we met in London. The glances she gets in the streets of Florence have not made her vain; they have made her feel more secure in herself. Feet are pattering up the stairs, the door opens and Julia is back. She collapses into the nearest chair, flings down her bonnet; she is clearly disturbed. Maria comes from the kitchen and runs a practised eye over her.

'What is the matter, *signorina*?' she asks, shapely buxom arms akimbo, one of them still holding a knife. 'Be calm; I will fetch you a drink.' From years of working for foreigners she knows well that they fail to drink enough in the hot weather. 'Here; drink.' She holds out an amber glass and Julia drinks thirstily, thanks her, and sits, not looking at either of them, bemused. Maria shrugs, returns to the kitchen. Janey sidles up to Julia and perches on the chair bedside her, rewarded by a welcoming hug. 'What is the matter?' she repeats in a whisper. Julia sighs.

'Oh just music things. When I got to the conservatoire today, they told me that Signor Bartolini was going to Milan and that I would have a new piano teacher. It's just the change; we've had a few changes in the last months, haven't we? I'd just like things to be the same for a bit.' And she sighs again, resting her head on Janey's shoulder.

'But our changes have been so good,' Janey murmurs. 'Please don't worry,' and she takes Julia's hand in hers, their roles reversed, she the comforter, Julia in need. Julia smiles.

'You are a dear girl; of course we'll be all right. I've just got to get used to the idea.' She gets up and goes to the piano. 'I've never had such musicians around me. I can hardly believe there will be somebody as good to replace him. I have to go back this afternoon after the siesta, to meet the new professore; he is meeting all his new students. He is from Rome.' She pulls a face at Janey. 'Probably far too good for me!' Janey shakes her head vigorously, curls bobbing; she puts her arms round Julia.

'Never, never!'

Julia laughs at such loyalty. 'It could happen,' she says, 'I think that's why I feel so nervous about the change. He may not like the way I sing - do you understand about subjectivity? Do you understand what that means?' The child shakes her head. 'Even though I get all the notes right and obey the text of the music, some people will still not like the way I play a sonata, others will. It's interpretation.' Janey wrinkled her nose, almost grasping the concept. 'This teacher may not like my playing. Signor Bartolini did. But this,' she added, placing the Beethoven book on the piano's stand, 'is the only thing to do meanwhile,' and she launches into the *Appassionata;* Janey settles beneath the piano so that the chords will vibrate through her body.

Later, when evening sun penetrates the shutters and the street's murmur signals the beginning of the *passeggiata*, Julia sits alone to read her letters. Letters to Florence have odd delivery patterns, and there is a bundle in her waxed bag. Always her father's first: wherever she is he is her constant correspondent: is she well, does she wear warm clothes, is she careful of her reputation, even writing to her in Guernsey, where she was sent to improve her cough, not to visit a man there who had a bad reputation with women. Almost an invitation! But this letter makes her sad, as he recalls his own days in Italy over thirty years ago, with Byron and Shelley, with Dina and Henry; halcyon days from an old man who will never get to visit again, who is now not feeling well and is missing her mother despite the presence of his youngest daughter Jacintha and her children. He loves and misses her and wishes she would write longer letters. Julia sighs and wrinkles her brow; she is so busy, practising and learning, he has long empty days alone with his pen. Next is Catherine Dickens; Julia is delighted with this as she thought her friend would still be overcome with the gloom of the collapsed marriage and its consequences. But no - she hopes Julia is well and is well herself: she has taken Miss Coutts' advice, had new cards printed and hired a carriage to call on her friends in the afternoons leaving them; she is surprised at the result, many callers and many invitations. Her new life has a pleasant routine, her own family, the Hogarths, are supportive, although she does not mention Georgina the sister who has stayed with Mr Dickens. She does not mention Mr Dickens. Hooray! thinks Julia. Shed him like a skin.

Miss Coutts' letter is in reply to one Julia sent, just after they arrived in Florence, thanking her for everything and outlining her studies. Miss Coutts writes with customary brisk enthusiasm, new plans, some proposed travel, although not to Italy. Please would Julia write more about the conservatoire as she loved to hear about women learning, and might find other musicians to send. Is the teaching what Julia wanted?

Julia folds all the delicate papers and replaces them in the bag. Her fingers encounter a small folded sealed letter which has slipped to the bottom. It's from Fanny. Janey will be so thrilled. Fanny writes that Tom is well and growing and has fallen in love; his object has huge brown eyes, glossy chestnut hair and a fine rump; they are inseparable. Julia smiles. All is well, so very, very well.

CHAPTER 18

If Music be the Food of Love...

The Count is forty, tall for an Italian, his thick greying hair a wavy mane back from his high forehead; broad shoulders becoming slightly rounded, a still slender neck and dark hooded eyes, the expression well-hidden when he glances downwards, following his straight nose, which is most of the time. He is sitting on a small dais at one end of the ballroom in the conservatoire, his long limbs stretched out in front of him; his clothes are sombre, black and greys with a white shirt finely stitched and bearing just a tiny scattering of pearls around the collar. Julia, seated with the performers at the other end of the room, reflects on how difficult that would be to wash; it probably gets unpicked and re-stitched at every laundering; or perhaps he just passes them all on to his valet, never wearing them again. The Countess, beside him, seems drained of life, her thin frame inhabiting her fine clothes like a visitor, dark shadows beneath her sad eyes. They do not speak. Grief for their only daughter is palpable, and this performance, in her memory, which seemed such a good idea at the time, is clearly taxing them almost beyond bearing. None of his houses nor all the money his family has gathered from centuries of papal gifts will ever bring them happiness now.

For this is the annual concert for the benefactors of the conservatoire. Their daughter, Guilia Maria Francesca, followed by many names from many grand Italian dynasties joined through careful marriage, died suddenly when visiting her uncle in Lucca when the typhoid epidemic raging in northern Tuscany hit the town; its mighty broad walls which had so successfully defended its inhabitants against foreign invaders were no match for the insidious infection of this mysterious killer.

The audience consists of other benefactors of the conservatoire, genuinely musical aristocrats who want to patronise musical Florence; others, less wealthy, teachers of voice and the piano from all over the city, gauging the latest talent, and parents and relations of the performers, which of course includes Claire, Janey and Paulina. There is a rustling of garments as people settle and converse in low tones, aware of the tragedy of this anniversary. It is early evening so the sun filters through the long windows, casting patterned light here and there and shadows as well. They sit in a semi-circle, spreading from the Count's dais, an arrangement seen in many great houses where composers and instrumentalists perform. This occasion sits uneasily between the domestic and the public. The head professore of the conservatoire rises and briefly outlines the progress of the concert. The

Count is known to want music not words. The tension in the air makes Julia's heart bang against her ribs. The singers go first, the pianists after. Guilia Maria Francesca studied both. Julia is the fourth singer. She has watched nervously as the Count has listened. He betrays no emotion, gently beating applause on his well clad long leg, his eyes down, his lips compressed. Claire squeezes her hand as she prepares to rise, Janey's eyes are huge with anticipation. Paulina stares straight ahead. As Julia reaches the piano and hands her music to the accompanist, a bird flies in at the open window, swoops through the room delivering a song the singers know they cannot match for purity, and disappears. The Count looks up, and before he looks down again his eyes settle on Julia. She is unaware; all her attention is on the music and her breathing. She fixes her gaze upon the left upper cornice of the room and nods to the accompanist.

Dido's lament fills the room, surprising the Italian audience with its restrained passion; their opera is dominated at present with Verdi and Mozart; the purity of the English Purcell momentarily startles before it thrills. Julia's voice is at its best; the warmth of Italy has rounded her deeper notes and Professore Righi has found a colour in it she did not know she possessed. An unexpected wave of home sickness overwhelms her as she remembers her dead mother and brother; as she reaches, 'Remember me!' tears are close but she keeps her voice firm for the descending phrases. The final descent of the accompaniment fades away and there is silence. The audience always waits for the Count to begin the applause; they wait. And wait. Eyes swivel from beneath coiffures and brows. Julia is in agony. Was it so bad? She keeps her eyes down, wishing she could seek Claire's for reassurance. She is rigid with fear, rooted to the spot. The accompanist is breathing hard, hands fidgeting in his lap. Suddenly she hears clicking, hard leather on marble, and has to look up. The Count has risen and is coming towards her, his hands outstretched for hers. He takes one of them between both of his and turns to the audience.

'*La signorina* has soothed our grief by her singing,' he says. 'My wife and I are always a little...' he stops and searches for the word, 'unsure - on this our Memorial Day, for the memory of Guilia. It rends our hearts, but today we have been soothed by this beautiful aria so beautifully sung.' The Countess bows distantly to Julia. The Count continues to hold her hand. His is a good hand to hold, warm and dry, the feeling light but firm. She leaves it where it is, curtseys to him with her other hand on her heart, incredulous at this attention, and the applause starts, rippling and echoing round the curlicued marble pillars. Finally it stops and he returns to his seat, she to hers. She hardly dares look towards him. His touch remains in her hand. So warm; was there a slight pressure?

***

When the pianists have followed the singers and the concert is over, Italian hierarchy re-establishes itself, no longer dominated by talent. The noble couple proceed to the salon next to the ballroom with the professori where snowy tables bear tiny crystal glasses of Marsala, a gift from the Count from his father's estates in Sicily. Everyone is invited, performers, teachers, parents, friends, and the company stands about deferentially as the Count moves quietly among them. The Countess has taken a seat by the window. Arriving at Julia's group, he smiles at Janey and raises a hand to drop a benediction on her blonde head. Julia wonders whether he is thinking of his daughter. He looks from Claire to Julia, to Paulina, puzzled by the relationships. He looks enquiringly towards Claire, who knows the form.

'Conte, this,' drawing forth Paulina, 'is my niece, Miss Clairmont; and my ward, Miss Julia Hunt; and her ward, Miss Jane Carter.' Paulina is the first to curtsey, her black eyes boldly seeking the Count's; Julia holds Janey's hand and they keep their eyes down.

'Miss Hunt,' he is well versed in patronymics and addresses. 'Miss Hunt, I - we - would be honoured if you would sing for us at a soirée next week. Now that it is hot we stay mainly in the hills at our summer house. In the evenings we have music; there will be others besides you, but you will be free to choose your own programme. But I insist you include the lovely lament of Dido.' Julia is utterly flummoxed, unable to speak or even to look at this overpowering man. Claire smiles confidently at him; she knows how things work in this city.

'It is an honour for my ward. Your highness would like...?'

'My secretary will make all the arrangements through Miss Hunt's professors,' he replies abruptly, as if quondam details bore him. He bows to the little group and turns away, leaving Janey wide eyed, Claire excited, Julia faint and Paulina snubbed. They talk desultorily in low tones with other students and teachers, until the sounds of carriage horses drift through the window; the Count and Countess are gone and the atmosphere lightens. Signor Righi descends on them with a broad smile and takes Julia's hands in his.

'*Cara signora!*' he cries, his delight palpable, his eyes alight, 'I am so proud! The Count is the most musical of men and he has chosen you for the Villa Dorsini! This could be the beginning of a great career here in Florence!'

Julia at last finds her voice. 'It will be different from my performances in London, I think. Can you tell me?' He puts her arm through his and draws her away from the group.

'I will tell you everything,' he says softly, 'and we will work and work until your singing is perfection. Carlo,' he winks at her at this presumptuous use of the Count's name, 'knows about music and we will make you so good that even he will find no fault. Or even the Contessa.' He raises bushy eyebrows. 'We must please her too, sad lady. Every day I thank the blessed Virgin that I have my children and pray for her who has none.'

They have arrived at his teaching room and he clearly has no intention of letting Julia go home with her family. 'What shall we give him besides Dido's lament? We will warm up, *mia cara*, and then do an hour.'

CHAPTER 19

The Villa Dorsini

Julia flings open the green outside shutters with a clang as the iron bar drops; they had left the inside ones open for ventilation in the night. She loves the rosy pantiled rooftops and the mingling of the different bells clanging across the city. When she is practising they disturb her ear and she has to concentrate hard to keep in tune, but at this time in the morning she loves them, making waves across the blue sky with the golden light spreading from the east. She turns back into the room where last night she had left her small trunk open for last minute additions; she goes in to the kitchen where Maria is preparing their modest breakfast. Julia hugs her, then perches on a high stool. Maria laughs.

'Why all this love, *mia cara signorina?*' But she knows really: nearly a whole week has been spent in preparation for Julia's departure for the Villa Dorsini in the hills. First Janey and Maria had attacked the wardrobe, both the gauzy daywear and the heavier performance frocks, Maria busy with alum and vinegar and lemon juice, freshening the heavier frocks and with lye soap, washing the undergarments and the thin frocks. Janey has meticulously studied every seam for signs of wear, and strengthened where necessary, replacing faded ribbons with new ones from the haberdashery round the corner, checking every button for signs of wearing threads. Julia had told her once laughingly of a concert in a great house where a soprano had attacked a high C with such force that a button on her bodice flew across the room much to the amusement of the assembled company. Janey frowns as she pulls and tests threads: no such thing was going to happen to her beloved Julia.

And then Julia herself; despite her twenty-nine years she needs little enhancement: she has her father's dark good looks with an unlined olive skin. Her hair shows no signs of grey, although she anticipates it will eventually, as her father is completely white haired in his seventies. They had dragged water up the stairs for her to have a hip bath in the kitchen; she swore this was unnecessary as she was fastidious about washing and had always lived in houses which were confined to wash stands and careful hygiene; she had washed, dried, combed and sponged her hair, rinsed it in vinegar with an egg to make it shine, and finally added rose water. Claire insisted on all this, and Claire knew about Italy and the arrangements in great houses.

For Julia is to stay a whole week at the Villa Dorsini. The Count has a big house party arranged and there will be entertainment every evening; he has a quartet, some soloists to perform with them, a very competent accompanist as there were singers other than Julia. So the musicians make up a small house party of their own and will be given the Count's choice of music to rehearse during the day. The professore is to go on the first day with Julia to arrange the music, and the Count has kindly asked if Janey would like a drive into the hills and then return in the evening with the professore to Florence. Julia is excited: the idea of spending so much time with other musicians thrills her, and the week in the Tuscan hills was more than she could have hoped for when she came to Italy. Claire is delighted at this turn of events and has no qualms about sending off her ward without a chaperone. She has governessed all over Europe on her own, unprotected, and despite losing her heart once or twice she only lost her virtue willingly to Byron and once or twice since when she desired it. She will give Julia some firm advice before she leaves.

Julia turns back into the cool room and smoothes the contents of the trunk before adding her last toilette accoutrements. Lowering the lid, she pauses and looks at its battered state. Should she be ashamed of such a shabby, antique item, bearing as it does the history of the Hunt family? She gently touches the worn canvas which shows the watermarks of the family's sea journey to Italy to join Byron and Shelley in Pisa; her hand moves to the locks which had accompanied and protected her father during his imprisonment in the Surrey Gaol, the event which, with the fine attached to it, determined the life of poverty the family has lived ever since. Julia smiles. Her love and admiration for her father, principled, gifted, generous and occasionally foolish, has burned bright all her life; musical too, for without his teaching she would never have started to play and sing, as lessons were out of the question when she was young and her brothers needed help to start on their careers. She fastens the lid firmly: she is proud of its battered look; it is perfectly serviceable, from the days when things were made well by craftsmen, rather than in a factory in Birmingham, and the memories bind her to home which she misses a little despite the excitement of Italy.

The Count will send a carriage at around nine o'clock, while it is still cool; the professore will come to the apartment and Janey is already sitting by the door in her best frock, clutching a little lace parasol. Suddenly there is a clattering of hooves as horses swing round the corner into their narrow. A coachman cries out to steady them, unused as they are to the confines. Maria's husband, Alberto, emerges from the bowels of the building to seize the trunk, ordered by his imperious wife, and the whole household runs down the marble staircase in a flurry of excitement. If the coachman found his surroundings less opulent than he is used to, he doesn't show it; he commands the groom to help Alberto load the trunk, then to hand in the passengers. The coachman cries, '*Avanti!*' With a great surge of horses, creaking carriage and harness, they are on their way.

Once over the bridge and out of the heat and bustle of the city, the traffic thins and the horses assume a steady trot which echoes as they climb the hills outside Florence. Julia is only half listening to what the professore is saying; her breath is truly taken from her by the blue hills and the mist which hovers;

she has never been outside the city since they arrived, and is totally unprepared for the beauty that is the bowl of this ancient landscape, blue sky and forests framing the great monuments, the pantiles glowing pink as the sun rises higher in the sky. Janey is hanging over the carriage door, her eyes wide with excitement, her hand flat on the outside of the door, feeling its heat and loving the smell of warm horse which drifts back towards her. She breathes deeply and remembers Tom in Essex, his new life dominated by horses and farming. She had seen him before they left England and loved the way he looked, brown as a berry, strong, smiling; she was glad she was as happy in her music and with Julia, so that their lives and moods were matched equally. How could they have possibly imagined this change? She looks over to Julia and her heart bursts with affection and pride.

Now they are clear of the city and trotting on dusty rough roads where branches hang low; sometimes the coachman slows the carriage and the groom gets down to move an obstruction; twice they have stopped to water the horses. Away from the road there are gleaming white buildings which seem to have no approaches, but the coachman raises his whip as he passes as if there are invisible gatekeepers lurking. Birds cheep in the hot stillness, the only other sounds being the horses' hooves and the click of cicadas. Julia and Janey exchange glances. The professore nods sleepily to the carriage's rhythm. Suddenly the carriage lurches to the right, hooves scrape on the rough ground, the coachman's voice calls out; they lurch again, then immediately they are on smooth ground, the rhythm of the horses re-established; Janey leans far out and can see the nodding heads of the pair, shaking occasionally to dispel flies.

'Look!' And she pulls Julia towards the window. They are trotting up a finely raked gravel drive which stretches towards a magnificent white villa in the distance. The professore has jerked awake and Janey bangs him on the knee. *'Guardi Signore*! Look at the villa! Or is it a *palazzo*?' She is not yet used to the distinction in Italian aristocratic houses; she knows her own is an *appartamento*, that the conservatoire has been a *palazzo*; that some of the great *palazzi* in Florence are still lived in by one family on many floors. But a great house in the countryside? The professore sits up.

'It is a villa,' he explains, his eyes following hers. 'In town it would be a palace; here it is a villa. A very fine house, as fine as his palace, but with fresh cool air for the summer when Florence boils.' He pulled a wry face. 'He has several, all of them family houses. But he is a good man, good to musicians and his family - such as it is.' He sighs and shrugs, reminding them all of the tragedy of the young contessa and her bereaved parents. He leans towards Julia. 'Perhaps that is why he wants our little girl today, so that the Contessa can have a child for a day? Sometimes I have brought my own youngest with me, and the Contessa gives them lovely days.' Janey begins to look uneasy, she had hoped she would spend the day with Julia and the musicians before returning to Florence in the evening. He catches her wary face. 'Do not worry, child - we will be sure you have an interesting day.' Julia is hardly listening; her eyes are on the gardens and fountains, the magnificent villa, the limonias and box hedges. The carriage stops. The professore becomes active, footmen are pulling out the steps and somehow they are all now on the gravel, dwarfed by the magnificence of the villa. The footmen help with the luggage, and the Conte is already coming out with the Contessa. Julia had not expected this, she had thought her status might have been nearer to that of a servant and perhaps a back entrance would be more appropriate. But no, they were in his carriage. It was confusing; her heart beats uncomfortably fast.

He speaks, in a mixture of Italian and good English, gently guiding Janey towards the Contessa, briskly issuing orders to the professore who seems to understand the form completely, finally turning to Julia.

'Miss Hunt: if you go with Signor Righi he will take you to the Music Room where the other performers are. Your trunk will be in your room for later.' He smiles, perfect white teeth with only a single snaggle at the side. She thinks it is good that he has at least one imperfection. 'Miss Carter will be happy with my wife: they will have a perfect day and will come to see you in the Music Room.' At this Julia nods at Janey and a little colour comes back into the child's cheeks. She seems to understand her role, and has already accepted the outstretched hand of the Countess. The Count turns suddenly away and disappears into the house. How raw it still is, thinks Julia, if seeing his wife take a little girl's hand almost unmans him.

The Music Room is a fine salon now murmuring with conversations, scales and occasional instrumental bursts. It is at the side of the house and looks over a limonia, where the warm citrus smell wafts in through the open windows. Now it is quite cool, being out of the sun, but the midday heat will soon catch it so any work needing to be done is best done before the siesta hour. Julia is introduced to Giovanni, the accompanist, sighing over the piano which he feels has not been tuned since the heat started to affect its strings, and the quartet which includes a young woman, Violetta; Julia notes that her frock is well worn and her body under nourished. I think she will be as glad to get this work as I am, thinks Julia. There is a baritone called Beniamino. With a mixture of Italian and English and professional rigour from Signor Righi, the musical content of the next few days takes shape. There seems to be a problem with the baritone; he should sing with Julia, as Henry would in England, but is reluctant for some reason. A spirited conversation takes place between him and the professore, no anger, enquiry from Beniamino, reassurance from the professore; Julia cannot understand the rapid Italian. Soon it becomes plain.

'Guilia, sometimes the Count likes to sing himself in the concerts.' He smiles at Julia's raised eyebrows. 'Do not worry. He is a trained and beautiful singer; he will sing about two songs alone; he is always modest about his abilities and respects professionals.' Beniamino nods. 'He has no need to be modest. You will see. But he may want to sing with you, or he may want Beniamino to sing with you. We will wait and see.' Julia needs to sit on a chair to digest this.

'He may sing - with me?'

'Maybe. Who knows? It is not a problem. We will work on everything he has asked for and a little more, then we can do anything he wants. Come, let us start, before it is too hot.'

CHAPTER 20

Art and Love

Later that evening, after a simple but palatable dinner with the other musicians, Julia returns to the room in the roof she is sharing with Violetta. It is hot but comfortable. 'They are good to musicians,' Violetta had assured her, while they were unpacking. 'This is like a holiday for me!' She explains to Julia that she plays violin at soirées and teaches days and evenings, and lives with her widowed mother and sick sister. Julia washes and tidies herself in preparation for meeting the Count to discuss music he may want to sing. The professor and Janey have been taken back to Florence. The evening is cooling a little as she threads her way down staircases and corridors, finally to her relief, arriving in the loggia where she is to be at six o'clock. She waits in the silence; there are distant voices and muffled domestic noises; cooking smells have escaped the kitchen as the main dinner is prepared. She glides noiselessly about, looking out of the windows at the grace of the gardens and fountains.

Suddenly, he is behind her.

'You have had a good day, *cara signorina*?' he offers quietly. Julia is startled. He is so different from his public persona, almost shy, deferential towards her. 'We have to discuss the music for the rest of the week. I think Righi has told you of my little indulgence.' He puts a hand beneath her elbow and guides her down the stairs and outside, towards the gently splattering fountain. 'Are you willing to sing with me? I will understand if you do not want to.' He turns away from her so that if she refuses she does not see his rejection.

'Conte, it would be an honour,' is all she can whisper at this moment. He relaxes visibly, takes her arm again and they walk away from the house, down a gentle slope towards the follies and little temples which grace the hidden corners of the garden. The evening is glowing from the day's heat and all sorts of creatures scuttle and fly about. Julia, town bred, can hardly name them, but she likes their presence and the warmth which caresses her skin rather than burns it in the midday heat. He starts to talk of Mozart and Verdi, he asks her closely for her opinion, describes to her performances he has been to, singers he admires, wants to know about London music, he has not been there since he was a young man. He has entertained Verdi in this place. Julia gasps.

'He has been here?'

The Count laughs gently at her incredulity. 'Yes, he has walked round this garden with me as you now walk! He will come here again soon.' He talks now of Bach and Scarlatti, she responds eagerly and an hour has passed before either of them realises. The evening is slowly dying to grey tinged clouds with pink peripheries and the moon is just visible. It is still warm, and the scents of the garden are all around them. Their walking brings them to a little temple with curved stone benches; gently he positions her before one and indicates that she should sit. The stone makes delicious warmth on her thighs through her thin frock as she tucks her legs beneath her. He hesitates, turns his head to one side as if requesting permission to sit beside her. She surprises herself by placing a hand on the warm bench, and he sits, beyond her hand, not too close, beside her.

'So you will sing with me?'

'Of course, of course. Anything.'

'Then let it be Mozart.' And they discuss the arias, the accompaniments; he strays from this and asks about her family, her life in London. She laughs and protests: it is too dull for him to know about. He wants to know how she arrived in Florence and how she lives. He is urgent, pressing in his enquiries; she is shocked by his interest. Another hour has passed before they reach the villa, candlelight spilling from the windows into the dusk. They are not the same people who left it. He has missed his dinner: that can be solved. But the turmoil within him is another matter.

***

Julia lies on her bed listening to Violetta's steady breathing. On the table next to her bed lies a flower she has found in her hair. The room is dark and very quiet, she feels as if her banging heart will wake the exhausted woman near to her. She tries to remember what has happened over the last two hours. She had prepared for a short, deferential discussion with a rather remote aristocrat; instead she has spent two hours with a man who proved vulnerable and shy, intellectually stimulating and musically gifted.

Her heart, that warm but wary organ, has opened to him and is open and aching now, how it was aching to be with him! Thinking of his dark good looks outlined against the fading light, she just longs to be back with him, for the talk, not for flirtation, for she had not flirted with him as there was no need; their hearts and minds had tumbled towards each other. Oh God, she thought, I have never felt like this, not with Edward or any of Henry's dear silly young friends, the many men she had met through her family and performances. It had always been fun, flirtatious, manipulative on both sides; she had never felt strongly about any of them and never sought their pursuit, quite happy to move on to another flirtation or entanglement, until Edward became so serious with her and her family pressed his suit. But the Count - *Carlo* she whispers to herself - made her heart race and she longs to be back with him, her mind and body for once in exquisite harmony, for she is not unaware of the quiver that goes through her whenever he touches her, however lightly.

But unobtainable. She takes the flower, and reaching for her waxed bag of correspondence, places it gently between the pages of her father's last letter. 'And how do I deal with this, old man?' she asks him. 'Always keen to advise me at every corner - what to do now?' Tears well up, and as she lies on her back paralysed with sadness, they trickle down into her ears.

CHAPTER 21

Challenges

Not looking her best after a sleepless night, Julia spends the next morning rehearsing with Beniamino the accompanist, and listening to the quartet prepare. Despite her inner sadness, she enjoys this; good music with talented people could never disappoint her, and she recalls talking to a young man at one of Thornton's soirées who described to her the thrill he got when he first went up to one of the universities and had serious discussions with likeminded people; this is the nearest she will ever get to that experience: in Florence at the conservatoire and here with these very good musicians. But the Count does not appear. How is she now to rehearse with him? Her heart feels broken, but she knows the performance must come first.

The door opens and the *maggiordomo* comes in with a letter on a silver tray. He murmurs to the young man who is the count's resident musician, who gestures towards Julia. A very slight bow accompanies the letter he offers her, after all she is not a servant but not much higher - and she blushes as she takes it. It is, of course, from the Count: he wants to rehearse with her later and suggests meeting at five o'clock. She thinks she must give this superior servant her answer, so glances up briefly and risks in hesitant Italian,

'*Va bene.*' Evidently that is correct procedure, for the man withdraws with another little bow.

Five o'clock and Julia is in the loggia caressed by a little breeze and clutching her music tightly to her. She has spent the afternoon preparing the texts of the duets he proposed; she has also managed a little sleep at siesta time; and meeting him is better than not meeting him, loving him as she most assuredly does. She is wearing a plain muslin frock of the lightest blue; she looks younger and the rather fugitive expression in her eyes gives her a vulnerability which is very attractive. The Count arrives and this time there is a familiarity between them; they are complicit without words in their decision to go outside, although she had expected to be taken back into the small salon.

'You are wondering, aren't you?' he says as they walk by the side of the fountain, flanked as it is by two reclining male statues, hips tantalisingly raised, 'Why we are not inside with the piano?' He laughs and whacks the air with his own sheaf of music. 'I love to sing outdoors, although I promise you we will practise with Beniamino too. I had heard,' and he smiles teasingly at her, 'I had heard that you too sing outdoors? In the streets with your brother?'

Julia takes a deep breath. 'How could you possibly know that?'

He makes tutting noises with his tongue and takes her arm. 'I have my ways! The music world is small and you have many admirers in London. I still have contacts there. There are not many women who sing in the streets and remain respectable. And I wanted to know why you do it, and how you came to the conservatoire. I wanted to know all about you.' She dares to look at him and asks why.

'Because, *mia cara*,' he replies, leading her into the House of Pan which from ancient times has stood in his garden, 'because...' and he seats her and stands before her; she is hardly listening but trying to make sense of it all while pondering his dark good looks and the allure of his figure. 'Because from the moment you started that aria at the conservatoire I wanted to know you and your music better. Somehow you spoke to my sadness and I needed so much to know you better. Now I do... a little... and I want more of you.'

Julia sharply remembers the occasion and the Countess who was with him. She is no fool and despite the love she feels for him is not going to become one; it is not possible that this exceptional man, this soulmate, can have honourable intentions towards a musician working as a servant in his house.

'Sir.'

'Carlo.'

'Carlo,' she hesitates, facing him honestly, although he has his back to the fading light so that his own expression is hidden. 'When I first sang to you, you were with the Contessa. I am a guest in her house; she has been kindness itself to my ward.' She pauses, wondering if he will understand her reluctance, and relieve her of the need to continue. But there is silence. 'I have had an evening of perfection with you, feeling...' she would say it but be careful, 'affection and intellectual respect I never thought possible towards a man. I too want to know more of you,' but she is overwhelmed and her voice fades. He comes to sit beside her in this House of Pan; perhaps the romantically disposed god, whose stony figure now grins at them, remembers other couples down the centuries. He pulls her silently towards him and she does not resist.

'I would expect nothing less than the fine speech you have just made, discovering as I have, the reputation you have for independence of spirit. You rightly remind me of Bianca my wife. I honour her and our lost child and would never desert her. I have deliberately in the last few years since our child's death been faithful to her beyond the custom of my peers, for I thought she had enough to bear, for I too bear it.' He pauses, and Julia is breathless for his sorrow. 'But then I met you and your loveliness, and your talented musicianship and your bright mind have reminded me of what I could have.' He stops. 'You see?'

'I do see. And I want more of you. I am not a paragon of virtue, as you must know if you have been enquiring about me; but I would not willingly cause sadness to another woman. How could we possibly know more of each other? My liaisons in England have always been with single men; but I know a writer who has recently taken a mistress and caused enormous sadness and upheaval to his wife of twenty years.'

'It's not impossible. I have many houses; you could live in one with Janey, and I can spend a lot of time with you, and we can sing together...'

'A kept woman? Everything I've been trying to avoid; I wouldn't be free. I'd be waiting for your next visit, hating your departures, longing for you, jealous of whom you might be with. And eventually you'd tire of me.'

'Never!'

'My voice won't last forever, my hair will go grey.'

'But this will happen anyway.'

'But at least I'd be free and independent and have teaching and friends and family, not dependant on a man who once loved me and has to continue to support me or not.' He puts a finger on her lips.

'You imagine too much, see too much into the future. At least think about it, while you still love me a little.' And he drew her out into the garden where a moon, not fully formed, made ghostly intrusion into the dusk. He passed her a re-arranged duet from *Così fan tutte,* she beat the time and their voices rose above the clicking of *cicale*. And then another song. And another. The singing stopped but it was a long time before they made their way back to the villa.

CHAPTER 22

'She never told her love...'

The performances during the week bring praise and applause from all the guests, some who are staying in the house and others from neighbouring villas. When Julia sings with Carlo there is naturally resounding applause, he is, after all, their host, but when she sings alone it is equally rapturous. After the concerts the musicians all withdraw to their own quarters while the guests have dinner, but Carlo and Julia manage to meet every evening. They do not leave the house as openly as they did when their relationship was innocent; he walks alone to the House of Pan as if clearing his head of the day's affairs, and she follows later as if desperate for some cool evening air. In the House the argument rages on.

'But I cannot live without you!'

'I do not want to live without you, but...'

'I will do anything you want! A house, education for Janey, I will make sure you have a position in society...'

'For me that will be a first.'

'The finest instruments to play on, the most beautiful gardens, your father can come and live here and renew his love of Italy.'

'Carlo, he can't even travel in London, be sensible.'

'You are the most ungrateful woman.'

'I'm not. But I have spent the last few years trying to be independent and I can't be anyone's mistress. I might have been your wife if we had met in another world because I love you and what we have together makes me happier than I have ever been before, and because I love you I would even have stretched it to having children - one or two - but I know deep down,' she banged her heart, 'that it is wrong, wrong, wrong for me to demean myself by starting a relationship such as you propose. It is nevertheless breaking my heart,' and she raised a tear stained face to him in the twilight.

'Demean yourself! I am the heir to…'

'Dearest, I don't care what you are heir to. That sort of thing doesn't matter to me. I've been avoiding marriage for years to a man who is heir to a very pleasant farm in England, who is a dear friend of my family. I can't suddenly become your mistress and say, 'But it's because I love him!' That's treacherous. I do love you, and we would have delicious times together, but what would I be? Not Julia Hunt, just *'la donna del Conte.'*

Carlo sighs like a furnace, and rubbing his hands together between his knees, he disfigures his handsome face making bellows of his cheeks. 'And what's wrong with being "the count's woman"? Many would be glad to be!'

'Don't continue with that,' says Julia warningly. He turns to look straight at her, narrows his eyes and stares at her.

'It is…' he pauses, trying to find the right English word, '*un ironia,* an irony that part of what I love most about you is what keeps you from me.'

'Then stop thinking of me as Susannah and you as your namesake in *The Marriage of Figaro*. Mozart's music is sublime but the antics offend me, and there is a Countess in it too.' He looks wounded and she tucks herself into his welcoming body. 'Carlo,' she whispers softly, 'my dearest, you have chosen the wrong woman to fall in love with. I don't want marriage or protection, and I have chosen the wrong man, for protection is all he can give me. But I know I would be in the depths of regret in years to come. And I don't want Janey growing up with me as a kept woman.' Carlo sighs and hugs her closer.

'I can't argue with you.' He breathes in her faint rose perfume, and kisses her neck. She shivers with delight. 'Stay here a little longer and I will try to battle with your undeniable logic. Until then, let's forget it,' and they stretch out on Pan's stony bench; the god is teaching them that love can be as uncomfortable as it is exquisite.

*

The days pass in a mist of fulfilled desire and further pleadings from the Count. Julia misses Janey but is glad that her existence is strengthening her resolve. She has her child, can have back her London, life enhanced by her studies in Florence; to leave Carlo will break her heart, is breaking her heart already, but her radical upbringing and the shoots of women's liberty that she has seen in England sustain her. She sees Carlo with the Countess, he is kind but distant; how long would it be before he was like that with her? In her villa on a hillside, thrilling views of Florence stretched out before her, waiting for his visits, servants who disapprove, neighbours who won't visit, no outlet for her music whatever he says; she has to keep these things at the forefront of her mind even when she is putty in his hands in Pan's secret House. Sometimes she thinks of Miss Coutts, protected by vast wealth but still alone and proud; sometimes of Catherine Dickens, starting out on the rocky road to independence after twenty years of protection by a man who abandons her; and often she thinks of Claire, thirty years on her own and unconquerable. Like these, her sisters, she will survive alone.

On the day of her departure Carlo keeps out of sight; she has requested this, unsure that she could mask her feelings if it was a public farewell. She curtseys to the Countess, who asks her to return with Janey. Julia says 'yes' but means 'no'. The carriage rumbles round to the front of the villa; she boards, waves, smiles broadly, leans back into its plush seating and weeps like an abandoned child.

CHAPTER 23

Reality

Julia has been back in Florence for a month; Carlo sends many letters pleading with her to reconsider: he is desolate without her, he misses her voice, her body, her presence. He mentions the size and position of the house he will give her, the musicians who would teach Janey and accompany Julia, he would pay professori to travel from Florence to continue Julia's lessons, she could have money of her own, jewels, clothes everything she wants or needs. His visits to her would not be solely of the flesh (she has to smile at his English at times), they would sing together, and the professori would train both of them in the latest Verdi arias; indeed she would meet the Maestro himself and could sing to him.

To a poor London girl, enduring poverty with cheerful nonchalance, longing to improve her considerable talents, you might say it was an unmissable opportunity. She thinks it through many times when the importunate letters arrive. She has Janey to consider too, and her needs, for she is a serious responsibility. She talks to Claire, in secret so the rest of the household does not know there is a crisis, or even an opportunity as some might see it. Claire tries to give a balanced response: she has had similar opportunities in her long career governessing in the houses of the European great; she has borne Lord Byron a child and ended up hating him with a passion for his part in the loss of that, her only, child. She has been saved from destitution by the generosity of Shelley in his will, and she well knows Julia's need for security. But she shares Julia's considerable reluctance to marry to gain that, so her advice is careful.

They are sitting in the little salon with the gently drumming footsteps of the *passeggiata* reaching them from the street. Julia sits on the floor at Claire's feet and is very intent on what is being said.

'*Mia cara*, you will always have a home with someone - you are blessed with your family and I will always love you and help you as long as I live. Edward still loves you and expects you to return to England and marry him...'

'But I won't marry him...'

'I know, I am just trying to see the possibilities! You love Carlo, which is more than most women do who accept the kind of offer he is making. So it is a better offer than most. But it is not you, Julia; you've seen the sacrifices women make to have children and security, and you've seen there are women who are trying to change this. You will never be happy perched on a Florentine hillside being visited by a man who eventually will make fewer and fewer visits, whatever he says. Dear girl,' and she reaches out and strokes the glossy head resting against her, 'think of Mrs Jordan - twenty years the last King's mistress, ten children between them, and then cast away when it was necessary to find an heir to the throne. And she dies in poverty in Calais, alone. Carlo might not be as callous as the English royal family, but it happens, and none of us can anticipate it.'

'That,' says Julia drily, 'I had forgotten.'

'I have always felt that if I was in control of my own affairs I could choose, and whatever situation I found myself in was my own choosing. After all, it was I who seduced Byron, not the other way round.' Julia's eyebrows rise; she gives a little gasp.

'And I always thought of you as a wronged woman!' Claire smiles.

'No. I'd been travelling with Shelley and Mary; they needed me, partly as a chaperone,' she burst into laughter at the thought of this, 'but also because I learned languages quickly and was fluent in French and Italian. They couldn't even bargain for a mule,' and she chuckled. 'But I wanted my own poet. It sounds ridiculous now but I was only seventeen! Everyone was in love with Byron and I was young and vain and poor.' She laughs unrestrainedly, black eyes glinting. 'When we got back to England I wrote to him and asked him to meet me at an inn; what man could resist such an invitation? I thought I loved him; he had not the slightest affection for me. But when our child was born I loved her with a passion I had not thought possible, and giving her up to Byron because he was her father broke me completely. Did you know your parents looked after her several times to help me? The greatest friends. Never underestimate their generosity to others, Julia; Shelley and Keats at times would not have survived without them; their kindness to me and Allegra saved my reputation. Damn Dickens for what he did to your family in that novel. It's the only book I have ever burned.' And her full mouth becomes a thin line as her gaze shifts away, seeming to see the flames that consumed *Bleak House* in her London fireplace.

'Another thing we have in common,' murmured Julia, 'but you hate two writers, whereas it's only Mr Dickens I'd like to kill.'

'I would never let another man wound me as I let Byron do over our child. I've grown old and Byron and Allegra are dead, and it's difficult to hate the dead as you hate them when they are alive, although my love for Allegra is the same. But I don't want you to make the same mistakes.' Julia rises and stretches to ease her cramped limbs.

'Thank you,' she says, *'cara amica*, I couldn't have had advice from a better source. If my happily married parents had tried to dissuade me I wouldn't have listened. And I expect my brothers would probably have tried to persuade me to accept! But what you say I understand. My heart always doubted; it is my body leading, and my ears, if you understand me. I'm going to kiss Janey goodnight, and then I'm going to bed to think.' Claire smiles as she watches Julia go to her maternal duties.

***

Julia stands by Janey's crib bed and cannot restrain a smile as she looks at the beautiful head framed by curly blonde hair. She leans down and kisses her lightly on the cheek; the girl stirs, opens her eyes and, seeing Julia, gives a half smile and goes back to sleep with the confidence of love. Sitting at the end of the bed, Julia feels there is really no dilemma: she is not mistress material and Janey should not be put in a precarious position. She will write to Carlo, in Italian, corrected by Claire, to make her meaning plain. She will tell him she loves him and will for the rest of her life; she will thank him for the exciting days she has spent with him; but she will decline the villa and riches he is offering because she is and will be independent. His final reply is simple: a large ruby on a twisted gold chain wrapped in a bank note for so many fiorini that Julia gasps; another note says: 'Go to La Scala!' Her eyes fill with tears. The grace of the man.

CHAPTER 24

La Scala

Their letters were always *Poste Restante* at the Post Office in Florence, and the custom of the English residents was to go twice a week, hardly more, for deliveries from England were slow, dragged over the Apennines by weary baggage horses or delivered by sea with its risks of delay by storms. So it was a long time after they were written that Julia received two letters from her brothers, Thornton and Henry, telling her that their father's health was deteriorating and that he had gone to his friends in Putney for a change of air in the countryside. It was really to tell her to address her letters to him there at the Reynells, so that there was less delay, because he waited so eagerly for them.

Julia is disturbed by these letters; her father is in his late seventies and has lived so frugally that he is fragile, thin, and always, in winter, at risk of chest complaints. She remembers him growing a flowing beard to keep his chest warm. The time she had bought at the conservatoire with Miss Coutts' money ends next month, and weather is approaching which will turn Florence into the annual inferno from which people of means flee into the hills around Fiesole. Claire hates this weather; but she has not the means to rent a house for all of them out of the Florence cauldron. She has friends in Fiesole who would welcome her on her own. Surely this is the time to put Claire first, and her father, and start the journey home? She will take Janey, and Paulina will have to stay in the apartment and get up to whatever she thinks fit. Maria will look after her until Claire returns.

Claire demurs but not for long. It is a relief not to have to face the heat. She will miss Julia and Janey, their company and their music, their improving languages which she watches over with rigour. They agree; they explain it to Janey, who will do anything Julia wants, and to Paulina, who receives it with more enthusiasm than she should; Claire must remember to remind Maria of the chaperone's duties.

Julia says goodbye tearfully to this lovely city where she has found music and love, friendship with her teachers, facility with a new language. She will leave forever the reminders of Carlo, his singing and his lovemaking in the little House of Pan, his lovely houses (for he had insisted she at least look at the villa that could be hers; it was unbearable and she wishes she hadn't), his perfect soirées and the talented musicians he gathered around him. Now she would never meet Verdi. But she would return to London a finer musician, a fluent Italian speaker and with greater confidence than she had ever had in her life. She can hear Henry saying 'Impossible!', but it is a different kind of confidence. She has turned her strong natural musical talent into well-grounded professionalism, and will be able to command higher fees for teaching and performing.

Julia and Janey are to travel overland and their journey takes them through Milan. Julia has decided that with Carlo's gift they will do what he, blessed man, intended it for. She has booked a respectable *pensione* near to La Scala and there are tickets available that night for *Rigoletto;* she knows from conversations at the conservatoire to avoid the stalls where everyone stands and the atmosphere is like a busy market. Janey is in the frock she wore to the Villa Dorsini, lovely in its simplicity, her childish blonde good looks drawing admiring glances. Julia, dark skin burnished a little by the Italian sun, makes a strange contrast in her deep red dress, the décolletage enhanced by Carlo's last gift. Can they possibly be related? Curious Italians speculate. The noise as they enter the foyer is deafening; the gamblers shout with triumph or howl with despair as their luck changes. Weaving their way between the tables Julia guides Janey up a staircase and in to their box near the stage, cheaper because of its slightly restricted view, but they can hear well as most of the noise in the stalls is behind them. They are cocooned in buttoned scarlet and gold, and Janey moves her chair closer to the edge and leans on the padded balcony. Julia watches her nose wrinkling as she breathes in the scent of flowers, the perfumed women and the strong undertow of sweat and alcohol rising from the stalls. Up in the *loggione* the devotees waft down their own smell - old clean clothes, fresh bread and cheese: these are the sternest critics and have made many a singer leave the stage. That is where I should be, thinks Julia. What pleasure to be where I am, and she silently thanks Carlo, missing him acutely.

Janey is simply entranced by the opera; her stillness and intent, unblinking eyes delight Julia, and she contemplates the gift the child has and how best to develop it. In the long intervals they discuss particularly Gilda's arias, and Janey asks such pertinent questions that Julia finds her a better companion than most adults would be. Janey is impatient with the intervals. 'Why can't they just get *on,* Julia?' she sighs, twisting the programme in her hot little hands, and Julia explains that a lot of people are just there to be seen and can't do without the pauses to eat or drink. Janey tuts and shakes her curls.

As the great curtains swing down and the singers take their bows, Janey joins excitedly with *'Brava'* and *'Bravo'*. Heads full of music they walk through the dark streets to their *pensione*; there are people about and occasionally from a group there is a burst of song. Suddenly, memories of London and Henry flood into Julia and for a moment she misses her family with an unexpected longing. The group in front take up one of the *Rigoletto* choruses, she joins in, softly at first and then louder. The group turns, continuing their chorus and she and Janey are drawn into the circle. They are music students, and admire her voice. She tells them that she has just finished at the Florence conservatoire and is on her way home to London.

'E la bambina?'

'She is my child,' she replies; and Janey beams.

CHAPTER 25

Changes

The peppering rain of a late summer storm beats on the roof of the train as it heaves its last hiss and roll into London; Janey's nose twitches slightly as she remembers the smells of her native city, pungently revived by the rain; Julia looks ahead for a cab to take their luggage, the small trunk too cumbersome for an omnibus; they will even have to have a porter. Suddenly, Janey cries. 'Look!' for her sharp young eyes have spotted a familiar figure, tall, thin Henry swaying towards them through the locomotive steam, wearing his cloak to keep dry; he descends on them like a bat and circles them both in his arms, and holds them tightly. And holds them. And holds, then lets them go but still holds their hands. Julia looks into his face.

'What?' She knows Henry so well, and he is not a good dissembler.

'Dearest, it's Papa.'

Julia's stomach churns. 'No better? How is…' but he pulls her head towards him, deep into his shoulder.

JULIA'S SHILLING

'He's gone, yesterday,' he whispers in to her hair. 'He just... died. No sickness, just slipped away, reading and writing to the end, loving the flowers and trees in Putney, they said, the Reynells, he just fell asleep in the garden. Thornton was there, he'd gone to visit and was in the house, but Pa was alone in the garden for a few minutes and then they found him. Thornton is devastated. To be there but to miss his going.' Julia starts to sob.

'Isn't it always the way, they seem to wait and slip away alone. Mother did it. Vincent did it too. I think it's to do with character, those who don't want a fuss.' Her tears flow.

'Weep,' said Henry, 'he is a man worth weeping for.' He looks at Janey, who has withdrawn her hands and is standing a few inches away. His paternal instinct makes him reach out for her hand which she gives willingly. 'Come here, little one,' he says gruffly, 'you understand our sorrow for you have known it.' It is exactly the right thing to say for it empowers Janey and she snuggles up to the weeping Julia. Henry tells them that they are to go to the Phalanstery, Thornton's house, where grief will be celebrated in the memories that the large household has of Leigh Hunt, and there will be comforting talk and tears can be shed mutually.

Suddenly Julia realises that Thornton, oldest child of Leigh Hunt, is probably now legally responsible for her. She is unmarried, fatherless and homeless. The cab they sit in is bearing all her worldly goods in her trunk and the girl sitting bravely beside her is her responsibility. The cab reeks of old leather, sweat and smoke; the clouds in the rumbling thundery sky are heavy with rain; London draws them in and she weeps, silently now, hardly comprehending the magnitude of her loss.

***

The burial at Kensal Green Cemetery is a sad affair; it rains heavily and they lurch between mud and puddles, clutching each other to stay upright. There are no women present, but all the men from the Phalanstery, the male children in the family over eighteen; very many literary London people, journalists, writers, musicians, with individual memories of this man's generosity despite his own poverty, his vivacity, grace and wit. They all agreed the inscription should be from his poem *Abu Ben Adhem:*

"Write me as one who loves his fellow men."

***

The dining room at the Phalanstery still bears marks of the building's former life as a school; the long table has little distinction as a piece of furniture, pitted with darker marks on its lighter wood; the odd large stains where some unloved mixture has lain, rejected even by strong young stomachs. Around the table there are at least fifteen unmatched chairs, and at both ends two carvers with arms, all in various stages of dilapidation. There are several candlesticks, some quite beautiful, but no candelabra, so the light is soft, dim, suited to the emotion of the moment. The conversation flows gently. It seems no time since Julia and Henry were singing here, when Claire made her suggestion that Janey should join the household. No time since Julia and Thornton had set off together to the house where their mother was dying. The children have eaten earlier and they have disappeared with Janey to hear her tales of Italy. *'Andiamo!'* she had cried, and they had trooped upstairs after her. Every now and then Janey will pretend she has forgotten an English word and will drop an Italian one into the conversation. Eyes grew rounder as tales grow taller.

Thornton and his wife Kate, her brother Arthur and his wife Susan, their aunts and cousins and uncle, sit long after the last pretty mismatched plate has been cleared, looking at Julia with concern. Her eyes are swollen and her plate had been untouched.

'My dear,' says her Aunt Bess, who sits next to her, 'it is a severe blow to all of us. He was precious to us all.' She dabs at her eyes and Julia could not helping thinking of Thornton's mild insinuations about her and their father. 'But we will manage, together. There is a place for you here among us.' Thornton leans forward in the old carver at the top of the table, flexing his fingers as he plays with the base of a flickering candle. The smell of roast meat still hangs heavy on the warm air, this August day.

'Indeed, dearest,' he adds kindly, 'I think you're my responsibility now, although I fear you do not relish that role.'

Julia is missing her father dreadfully; she had no idea grief could be so all pervading. When her mother died she had not had this awful, grinding heartache which will not go away; she had been distracted then by her need to care for her father as the unmarried daughter. But this, this daily horror she must bear alone, of waking and thinking it hasn't happened, then the sickening thud in the stomach which tells you it has; she was not prepared for this. Every night before she sleeps her mind is filled with images of him as he was, all his kindnesses, his uncomplaining acceptance of her ideas and sometimes bad behaviour. Sometimes she re-lives the times when she truly shocked him, when she was profligate with money and distressed him. She feels his presence beside her and sees his hands on the piano, teaching and guiding. She feels she will never lose that presence as she plays.

She feels the anger of grief. She glares at Thornton from beneath wet lashes; has it come to this, after all her efforts to maintain herself, that she is to become her brother's *responsiblility*? Two cousins, further down the table, dark heads together, murmur to each other; accepting as they are of Thornton's protection and indeed his generosity, it is not their first choice in life. They know Julia from childhood; they doubt she will slip easily into the role of dependant, another single woman with little income. For a fleeting moment Julia thinks of Carlo, and his offers; but she dismisses him from her mind. Common sense establishes itself and she tries to speak steadily.

'That's kind, Thornton, all of you. I am grateful for everything you are doing for me and Janey.' The cousins have brought coffee from the kitchen and are busy pouring it into cups, some where the light flickers through, some thicker, with or without saucers. Julia takes a cup and hangs onto the saucer, as if seeking its helps for her shaking hands. 'I will be glad to stay with you all for a few days while Jacintha sorts out Papa's house. She is happy to have me there to help with the children, but I will be grateful to stay here, while I clear out there, and try to make some order for me and Janey.' She senses humour in the air.

'I know order is not what you usually associate with me,' and she smiles for the first time in a week, 'but I know I do need to sort things out now that Janey is my responsibility. I—'

'But dear Julia,' breaks in Kate, Thornton's wife, 'Janey has a home here, she can stay as long as she wants, and so can you, it's so simple. We need help with teaching the piano to the children who are getting beyond us, and you are so good with a needle, and your ironing is better than mine.'

'I will always teach the children the piano, as long as you need me. It will be my pleasure and I'll fit them in with the other pupils I teach. My studies in Florence have made me a better musician in every way, just as Miss Coutts intended, so I'm able to teach to a higher standard, I may even get work at the Academy. My performances will be better too, and I am resolved not to sing outdoors any more. Papa didn't like it and I'm not sure it's a good example to Janey. Henry and I will get real engagements now.' She pauses, and places the saucer carefully beneath the cup, with the smallest chink. 'You see before you a daughter reformed by new responsibilities, to herself and her ward.' Such a startling idea makes her smile again. She gets up and goes to the head of the table to Thornton, and standing behind him she embraces him, her head leaning on his. 'So you see, my dear, you don't have yet another female dependant,' she realises that this is a mistake and raises both hands apologetically to the women around the table, 'but an independent woman with good skills determined to live on them. But you are a good, kind brother and I honour you for that.' Releasing him from her arms she kisses the top of his balding head and sits back in her place at the table. Thornton frowns; he is puzzled. Never has he had an offer like this from a woman. Tentatively he says,

'That is all very well, Julia, but you may be short of money.'

'And you cannot live on your own!' expostulated Bess, her voice rising in anxiety. She's so like Mother, thinks Julia, in looks and voice, but not in spirit; she would never have stood up to Lord Byron when he called her children dirtier and more mischievous than Yahoos; she would have been subordinate to his nobility. 'It's not seemly! Are you going to marry Edward? No of course you're not, or you wouldn't be talking of working and charging fees! Where will you live? You've always been wilful, Julia, from the time you were a small child. Think what your parents would want you to do, they'd want you to stay with Thornton and us!' Julia narrows her eyes and raises her well-marked eyebrows. She lets out a long breath. This is not the time to have a row with her aunt. Her new way is to be calm and take charge. She will just keep repeating her plans. The candles gutter and the light outside fades; more coffee is brought, a glass of wine for the men; Bess faintly asks for wine too. Julia laughs inwardly: she is attempting a little blackmail. One by one they retire to bed, doors softly opening and shutting as they check children and take their candles upstairs. Only Julia and Thornton remain.

'I mean it, old boy,' she says, taking his hand across the table. 'At least let me give it a try. If I fail you can have all the satisfaction of scooping me out of the gutter and bringing me back to your little paradise!'

JULIA'S SHILLING

'And you won't marry Edward?' Thornton's lean lined face lights up as he looks at her. He can remember holding her as a baby and wondering how his middle-aged parents could go on producing children. He had loved her then with a boyish ardour for her dark curly head, deep brown eyes and flushed baby cheeks; he had loved her less in his teens when her toddler tantrums disrupted the whole house and only her father could soothe her hot tears with music and kisses; and now he loves her because she knows him so well, is tolerant of his weaknesses, of which she does not approve but neither does she judge; and she is quite simply the most unusual woman he knows.

'No, I won't,' she says firmly, squeezing his hand. 'He expects it because he thinks I'm destitute and will want to help the family; I am destitute, but Claire has survived and so will I.'

'But Claire had money from Shelley,' sighs Thornton, 'and I don't think you have any loving benefactors lurking in your cupboards.' Little do you know, she thinks, but never will I share with anyone my love for Carlo and his offer to keep me. 'But I was talking to Bryan Procter after Father died.'

'Procter?'

'Yes you know him, he knows everyone, like Father, and he said you had been to see him and his daughter and they hoped you would come again, but...'

'Oh,' says Julia, 'I always think of him as Barry Cornwall, the name he writes his novels by. Yes, I should have gone.' She pulls a wry face as she remembers the calls she has often failed to return for some livelier offer.

'Before he started writing he was a solicitor and he feels that as Father's only surviving unmarried child you possibly have a right to part of his civil list pension. He even said that if you didn't get it he and others would create a private pension for you.' Julia is incredulous.

'What wonderful people! I had no idea men could be so altruistic.' She stops, horrified. 'They are being altruistic? No strings?'

'Absolutely altruistic,' Thornton states firmly. 'No strings. How could you possibly think such a thing?'

'Easily,' smiles Julia, 'but let's leave it. Such kindness is rare but I'm not sure I could accept it.'

'You probably won't have to,' replies Thornton. 'Procter and his friends make an appeal to the government and a minister decides. It wouldn't be the whole pension, mind you, just a percentage.'

'If it was mine as father's daughter I would feel honoured and independent. And whatever it is it will certainly be better than—'

'Being scooped out of the gutter and brought back to live with Aunt Bess' plans for you? And ironing better than Kate?' He laughs, stands up, stretches and hugs her. 'It's late. Let's hope it works. I have to be in early tomorrow, the journal is put to bed by midday and then I have more things to do.'

'See Mrs Lewes?' says Julia naughtily. Thornton frowns at her then has to laugh. 'You have no respect!' he replies quietly.

'And you have all those extra children!'

'I love them all!'

'So you should!' And she kisses him and makes quickly for the stairs. That night the weight that has been sitting on her chest is a little easier, and the images of her father are all benign.

CHAPTER 26

Mrs Dickens' Surprise

Julia is back on Miss Coutts' doorstep; the doorman who opens it bows gravely and walks ahead of her up the beautiful staircase, but before she can reach the top, Blossom, the spaniel, hurtles down it and jumps up, trying to reach her face like all small dogs do. She bends down so that she can take the little paws between her fingers and mutter endearments in the curly ears. From above Miss Coutts can be heard remonstrating mildly in the tones of the completely devoted, and when Julia enters with the dog in her arms she hugs them both.

'My favourite girls!' She is beaming and holds them tight. What a difference this is from my previous visit, thinks Julia, when I was almost too nervous to accept her generosity, and could hardly distinguish a footman from a butler. She becomes aware of another person in the room: Catherine Dickens sits hugely in a chair by the window, leaning heavily on a stick, but her dress is fashionable, her eyes bright. Miss Coutts draws Julia towards her.

'I've heard you've had a very good time in Florence,' says Catherine. Miss Coutts smiles at Julia.

'I have many friends who know the Florence musical scene well and I gather you were a tremendous success.' I wonder what else you've heard, thinks Julia, but decides it does not matter. She sits next to Mrs Dickens, who prefers to remain seated, owing to her increased weight.

'I had a very good time indeed. I can never thank Miss Coutts enough; being in Italy transformed my life; my music has improved, I can speak Italian, I seldom cough now because of the sun, oh, it was all so wonderful!' Her face is flushed and the other two women join in her pleasure.

'She is good at transforming lives, isn't she?' says Catherine to Julia, waving her fan in Miss Coutts' direction. 'Very good. Look at me! I have a bad leg because I put on weight because I eat too much, but then I have such an appetite! No Charles to disapprove every time I take a forkful! And I don't care! I'll hardly die young. Every day I can decide where to go and what to do, I had no idea living alone could be so good. I have the servants, of course, and Miss Coutts shamed Charles into such a reasonable settlement that I can enjoy myself as I please. And to think how I was weeping on the sofa when I last saw you! And you, Julia, will you marry Edward now? Think carefully, my dear, there's a lot at stake!'

'I certainly will,' but Julia decided to keep off that subject as things were fragile there, much as she would like to explore this astounding statement from Catherine. 'I've had good news. My brother Thornton told me yesterday that the government has approved that I become an annuitant - that I get a third of my father's civil list pension, for the rest of my life! That does change things for me.'

'It certainly will,' Miss Coutts adds drily. 'It moves you from dependence to independence. Money changes everything for women. They are even talking of letting women keep control of their inherited money within a marriage now, but it will be a long time before it happens. Is it enough for you to live on?'

'No, certainly not, but it will provide the basis, so that I don't have to join Thornton's happy band at the Phalanstery. He's so kind to them all, and they're so grateful, but I'd end up having differences with Aunt Bess on everything, and disagreeing with Thornton about his second family with Mrs Lewes.' Catherine sighed at this; it had bothered her but it didn't seem to bother Agnes Lewes. 'If you hadn't sent me to Florence I wouldn't be so well equipped as I am to earn,' and she turned to Miss Coutts and hugged her. She fished in her reticule and took out a tiny embroidered pin cushion she had bought in the via Romana from a little shop run by a mother and daughter. 'This is to say thank you.' Miss Coutts is pleased. She appreciates simple thanks; a greater gesture would have embarrassed her.

'So what are your plans? Have you had time to think?'

'It's not just me; I have Janey to consider as well.' She briefly explains Janey to an astonished Catherine. 'I want to rent some rooms, probably near my family in Hammersmith because living is quite cheap there, and I can earn the rest of what is needed, singing, teaching, even teaching Italian to singers. Janey will go to school, and I'll teach her piano and singing.'

'Janey will come within my education fund,' says Miss Coutts.

'So you'll have a child,' says Catherine ruminatively. 'You'll have everything, money, a home and a child. What more could anyone want?'

'An interesting occupation,' replies Miss Coutts severely, 'she needs something to do. And she has that.'

'But you are single, Julia,' adds Catherine, 'isn't living alone a problem for a single woman?'

'It has never bothered me,' says Miss Coutts firmly, 'and that's because I have lots of money - lots and lots of it - so now that Julia has a little she can do as I do. Women need money and education; it's what men have and Julia has both now.' A little gold clock strikes the hour somewhere in the room. Julia jumps up.

'You will have to excuse me, I have to meet a lawyer about the pension.' She kisses them both and strokes Blossom's whiskery chin. 'I'll be back to see you soon!'

When she has gone the two remaining women stare at each other.

'Things are changing,' says Catherine.

'Thank goodness,' replies Miss Coutts, as she looks out of the window to the street where the little prostitutes are gathering in the dusk.

CHAPTER 27

Boundaries

'You what?' growls Edward, sotto voce, his straw hat tilted over his nose. They are sitting beneath the coppery shade of an ancient beech tree in the garden in Essex, backs almost to each other and he keeps his voice low because below them in the paddock Janey is sitting on a piebald pony which is being led by Tom. In his country clothes he looks as if he had been born on this farm; he is muscular and brown, unrecognisable from the skinny boy in tattered clothes Julia found in London. Julia's thin frock, stitched for the Italian summer, is too thin for the approaching autumn and she shivers slightly. Edward shifts to put his arms round her, and whispers again, 'What?'

Julia sighs, coughs and takes a deep breath. 'I'm going to take some rooms near the Broadway, not far from where we used to live in Hammersmith in fact. I've found three rooms with a smaller room for the kitchen. They're upstairs in a house a bit like the one my parents lived in, not far from Jacintha and her brood and close to Henry and Dina. It's quite respectable being near one's family.' She laughs.

'Not as respectable as being married and having a husband to protect you!'

'Not sure what this protection idea is all about,' murmurs Julia. 'All the women I know who live alone just need money to pay the rent and buy food and clothes. What is this protection you're talking about?'

'It's what you need from a man! It's very dangerous for a woman on her own! Don't think you won't be preyed upon by unsuitable men if you live in lodgings.' Julia thinks for a minute, then pauses to appreciate better Janey's progress on the pony.

'Look Edward, how quickly she's learning! I wish I could do that!' And she claps softly and waves. Janey nervously removes one hand from the reins and waves back. Tom firmly replaces her hand and they continue the lesson. 'I think I can manage the unsuitable men; the door will have a lock and I've been able to look after myself for a long time now,' and she kisses his hand lightly, chuckling as she does it. 'You know that perfectly well. You were prepared for me to do very unconventional things with you as long as I was under my father's roof. I assure you I will continue to do them with you as long as we both want to; you're worried about losing me. You won't. I'll just be living somewhere different.'

'But if we marry you could be living here with my family and Tom would have Janey here and Aunt Fanny would help with raising our children, and you'd have more money than you can possibly make from teaching and this wretched pension. I wish they had never given it to you!' Edward tears off his hat and hurls it onto the carpet of last year's beech leaves which lie mouldily around them. Julia laughs at his petulance.

'Do not speak disparagingly of my pension,' she teases. 'I'd rather not have it in a way, I'd rather be able to earn lots of money and do without it, but given that it's there it's a very real buffer to my earnings, and in case I get ill.' She coughs slightly as if to remind him of the need to keep it. 'Edward, you don't seem to understand the depth of my need to be on my own and do my music. I've seen what babies do to women, and I'm so lucky to have Janey, and Tom. Without them I might seriously consider marrying you, lots of women marry just to have children, for it expands their lives for ever, but now I have Janey to love, and I love you, as long as you'll put up with me.' Edward groans and stretches full length on the leafy ground, covering his eyes with his arms. If only he could do without her. Women are easy enough to come by, but not her sort of woman. That's her attraction.

They get up and walk towards the paddock; Tom has let go of the leading rein and Janey walks the pony slowly, straight backed, moving gracefully.

'She's a natural,' he says, 'she just sits right and knows what to do with the horse. If she stays a few weeks I could have her riding like a hunting lady.' He looks quizzically at Julia, studying her face, swishing the long grass with his whip. 'Could she stay?' Edward replies, it is after all, his family home, and he sees an advantage.

'Of course she can, Tom, as long as she likes. I can see that you'd both like to be together, and she may become as good a rider as you.'

'No,' says Julia firmly, stepping forward as Janey returns to them, patting the pony's neck and holding the bridle so that Janey remains in the conversation, 'No, thank you, it's kind of Edward to say that but Janey and I have to move in London and Janey has to start lessons and do her music. She is talented like you, Tom, but with music and languages, and she needs to be with me in London to do those. We will visit as much as suits Aunt Fanny (a good point here, thinks Julia, as Aunt Fanny is really the host), so that Janey and you will always be together.' Tom smiles at this reassurance. He loves Julia, and sometimes if he has not fallen straight asleep from outdoor exhaustion, he thinks of the cold night in London when he tried to pick her pocket, and her response to his robbery being to give him money. Never, never will he forget his path to his now idyllic existence. Janey looks down on the group - the pony is fourteen hands high - and nods.

'I'll ride every time I come here,' she says to Tom. 'But you know I have to be with Julia. It's that or service,' she ends dramatically. 'That's what girls do, work their way up from scullery maid to be parlour maid and I'm not doing that. Working from six in the morning until ten at night, I'd never sing a song or read a book again.' She hands the reins to Tom and dismounts. Good God, thinks Edward, she sounds like Julia already. Tom and his sister walk together towards the house with Julia and Edward following. The sun is dropping behind the house and bathing it in a golden light. So beautiful, thinks Julia, like Carlo's house, but with similar trappings. Not for me.

CHAPTER 28

Freedom

The rooms are clean and bright, Mrs Hornton, the landlady, pleasant and civil. If she is curious about Julia's status with a child she does not show it; Julia has looked at the rooms with Henry and Dina and having her brother around seems to be enough reassurance. She accepts that she is Miss Hunt and that Janey is Jane Carter. The size of Carlo's bank note has left money over for when Julia returned to England, because a lifetime of frugality cannot be abandoned in an evening. The *pensione* near La Scala was modest, their activities in Milan inexpensive and achieved on foot. So the first month's rent is paid, and she has also bought a good upright piano, which has amused Janey with its curly walnut patterns and the even curlier double bracket candles which grace its upright case. Julia has severely tested it with some difficult Beethoven and fast Mozart before handing over the money she has agreed to pay the old man, an acquaintance of Mrs Hornton's, who is selling it. He lives nearby, a retired musician whose rheumatism has ended his career. The departure of the piano and the arrival of the money he views with equanimity; at least, for the moment, he won't starve. He likes Julia and admires her playing; he is glad it is going to a good home, and he recommends a local tuner. Julia realises she has forgotten this regular expense, but she will manage. Bread and water some days, she says to Janey, who is sufficiently secure now to know it's almost a joke.

'We will keep in touch,' says Julia to Mr Sandford, 'you must come and hear Janey play and tell her to keep her foot off the pedal!' Janey blushes; she hates getting things wrong.

Seeing this he says, 'It's always a problem with young learners - size of the feet I think.'

'Probably,' agrees Julia cheerfully, 'but don't give her too many excuses.' They laugh together, telling him they will send her brothers round with a hired cart to move it; he is not surprised; only the rich employ removal firms. At the same time they will move her belongings and some furniture from her father's former home.

***

Julia is sitting at her father's old writing table, which her brothers have generously allowed her to keep. The sun is shining into the south facing room, splashing the busts of Shakespeare and Milton which have taken up familiar positions on an old bookcase, dizzily peering down into the room; she looks closely at them, noting at least two new chips from their short journey from her father's house; but having survived the sea journey to Italy and their sojourn in the Surrey Gaol all those years ago she is almost pleased now to have put her own mark on them. Her father had always created around him a room full of books, paintings, statuary, battered and fragile, and flowers - that was what is missing, she thought, we have no flowers. She leans back in the creaky chair and looks with satisfaction around the room; all these objects have been touched by him and my mother; she runs her hand over the desk and loves knowing that his hands have been on it day after day for so many years. The ink stains and chipped wood where he would sharpen his quill before steel pens came in make her smile. She can never understand people who want everything new, like Charles Dickens, when they start to have money; the memories of even this very modest inheritance give her pleasure, and she had noted Miss Coutts had an eclectic mix in her house.

Whatever happens, she thinks, the annuity will cover the rent in this sort of accommodation, and we shall feel secure with these things around us. Everything else I will have to earn. I can have more modest pupils here, and if I go to wealthy pupils I will adjust the fee to include the cab fare. Italian will be extra, and only for the purposes of singing: she was not confident enough to offer full Italian lessons. And then I will do the soirées and other performances. It should all work, and there will be enough for both of us. Janey is on the floor on an old Turkey rug, also part of the inheritance, poring over a score.

'Come here,' Julia says, 'you might as well know what it is all about.' She has a sheet of paper in front of her and a well sharpened pencil. 'You know I'm not the best organised person but if we want this to work, we both have to be.' Janey draws up an old upright chair and peers at the paper. She does want it to work. Julia explains the rent, the annuity, the calculation for food and laundry and clothes; she asks if Janey can think of anything else they will need.

'Do candles and coal go in with food?' she asks. 'We do use a lot when we practise and read. My mother always found they cost such a lot.'

'Good girl! I had completely forgotten! The short winter days and the cold nights. That's a lot of money I hadn't calculated for. A lot of your clothes will have to come from the other families - do you mind very much?' Janey did not mind. She still had vivid memories of tattered, dirty clothes when she and Tom lived beneath bridges and in filthy doss houses. The clothes from Thornton's and Dina's children were always pretty and well worked over to fit her precisely. Certainly she did not mind.

'Mine will be as before, gifts from the rich and anything colourful I can find in the second hand trade. You can't believe how little rich women wear a dress before they tire of it. And their maids have first picking and then they sell what they don't want and that's where I get my best things. We'll be the smartest people in town!'

***

The next day Janey sets off for Thornton's house; it has been agreed that she should go there for lessons when his children were taught by their many relatives. This would save Julia the expense of a school and she knows Janey will have better teaching than at most girls' establishments. Julia has a pupil in Kensington and will take the omnibus there. She meets Mrs Hornton at the bottom of the staircase.

'Are you getting comfortable, Miss Hunt? Is there anything I can help with?' She anticipates that this one woman and one child will be quiet and careful tenants; the three rooms would normally attract a family, and that could not only grow but be noisy and troublesome. So she is keen to help.

'We are indeed, Mrs Hornton,' Julia replies. 'But if you hear of any china for sale I would be most grateful. My father had little left after a lifetime of use, and he rarely replaced household things.' Mrs Hornton always knew when things were surplus to requirement or needed to be sold to raise money among her neighbours.

'I'm sure I'll find you something. Are you going far today?' Julia didn't mind the enquiry; she wouldn't be hiding anything as she intended to keep her relationship with Edward strictly on his premises, for Janey's sake as much as Mrs Hornton's.

'I have a pupil, actually two, in Kensington. They're sisters, but at different stages so I teach them separately.' The landlady purred, illiterate herself, she had respect for learning and loved music; she had heard Julia practising, both piano and singing. There was nothing else to entertain her in the evening so she was pleased to listen.

'When you sing out, Miss Hunt, and go to all those great houses.' Julia thought she might have slightly exaggerated her engagements, but she supposed Miss Coutts might be classed thus. 'I can always look to the little girl.'

'How kind,' Julia replies. 'I had thought I might ask you later and that we could come to some arrangement...'

'No need for money. I shall enjoy her company. I haven't any of my own. We were never blessed.' Tears start in her eyes. 'Everyone else having more than they could feed and us with never a one. That's why I have the house. We never had anyone to spend our money on.' She brightened. 'So I will be glad of the company. Just let me know. I'm rarely out of an evening.' Julia touches her lightly on the arm.

'You're so kind,' she says. 'That will really help.' Touching her again briefly she lets her open the door and sees her off towards the omnibus. *She's a brave woman*, thinks Mrs Hornton, watching her disappearing into the distance. *Whatever her story is, I don't mind.*

CHAPTER 29

Simply Pleasure

Edward is finishing the last woodcut for the *Illustrated London News* when he hears her light footsteps on the creaking stairs. It is winter now and the fire in the grate burns bright with the wood shavings he feeds it with as he works. He has tidied up the studio in anticipation of this visit; since having her own rooms, Julia has become less tolerant of what passed for artistic licence, so the cheese is covered with a cloth, the bench swept of crumbs and the tea leaves emptied; he has brought up from the well downstairs fresh water and made the sofa tidy with plumped up cushions. God alone knows, he thinks, why she has suddenly become domesticated; when he visits her he never stays the night but he can see it's clean clothes and sheets changed every week, food cooked carefully or from the landlady's kitchen. His handsome face darkens. He knows really. It's because of the child; Julia has grown up because she has Janey to look after. He quite resents being sent home at the end of the evening. He senses Mrs Hornton, who finds him quite captivating, would be happy to turn a blind eye if he stayed. But Julia has made it plain that it suits her to come to him for what she laughingly calls the visits of the flesh - wherever did she learn such an expression? - so that Janey is not troubled by adult passions.

Suddenly, she is there, her bright face and cheerful voice filling the room and dispelling his gloomy thoughts. She kisses him lingeringly on the lips, draws off her gloves and shawl and sinks into the sofa.

'I really look forward to my visits of the flesh,' she murmurs, pulling him down bedside her. 'Less is better!'

'Where *did* you hear such an expression? It's terribly male!' Julia realises she has said more than she should, for she has never told Edward about Carlo.

Fixing her eyes blankly on the fire, she says dismissively, 'Oh, it's the Italians, you know, they call a spade a spade. Just something I overheard.' Edward seems relieved.

'A good day?'

'Yes,' she replies. 'Janey spent the morning with the aunts doing arithmetic and English; I visited the Misses Bailey in Kensington and earned a guinea for the morning's teaching; you know, I arrive in a cab, which I charge them for, and I really think they like it better than me walking to them or going on the bus! They find it more respectable. If only they knew!' She snuggles up to him. 'And then I had two pupils at home in the afternoon and Janey joined in the lesson; she's almost better than both of them already. And

JULIA'S SHILLING

Mrs Hornton sits on the stairs and listens! What she might have achieved if someone had taught her to read and write and sing and play! She had six brothers and money was tight and naturally it went on them.' Edward sighs. He thinks he may have to wait to get her into bed while she develops her thoughts on the injustices men inflict on women. He's right.

'It all comes down to money, Edward, and education. If women have money and control of it they're not trapped by marriage and child bearing; if they're educated they can earn their own. Do you think men have deliberately deprived them of both by passing laws which prevent them having either? Come on, tell me Edward, you're a man, you must know.' She is becoming very animated. He sighs even more deeply. This was not how they were meant to spend the evening. And he really hasn't an answer; like most men he simply accepts that life is better and freer for men and that women provide family life if they marry men with some money, and are sources of pleasure for men if they don't. It can't be changed. It's how things are.

'I don't know why you want to work and live alone,' he grumbles, 'when you could have leisure, comfort and security with my family. I…'

Julia interrupts. 'It's not all about me. It's all the other girls growing up like Janey. I want her to be able to *choose,* like men do. I know *poor* men can't choose to be educated, but they still rule their families and have other advantages, like not being constantly with child and escaping from their children in the day.' Edward is about to point out the joys of motherhood and the leisure a woman enjoys, but thinks better of it. It will only prolong the discussion. Can't she just stop thinking and get on with their lovemaking? Suddenly, he is aware of her bright black eyes on him.

'I know what you're thinking,' she laughs. 'Why can't she shut up and get into bed with me? Isn't that what she's come for?' Edward, you make my point for me! But I love you and love coming to you, and love my life at present, probably more than you love yours. I treasure mine the more because I never thought I'd have it. You were born to education, money and independence.' She stops, smiles and kisses him. He gives up, seizing the day. He takes her in his arms, loosening her laces and unpinning her hair. He'll do whatever she wants, for as long as she wants. She shakes her long hair but before enduring the elderly sofa, she says, 'Is it really possible that men have conspired for hundreds of years to prevent women being independent? Surely not! No one would do such a thing!' And laughing she joyously hugs him to her.

CHAPTER 30

1872

Jane attended Julia's funeral at Kensal Green cemetery, despite the conventions, but times indeed are changing and she has persuaded Thornton that she should. Thornton is not well himself; long hours as editor of the *Daily Telegraph* have weakened him; his children have grown up and he and Kate now live alone near Euston Square. Jane did not want Julia's last journey to be without her. Tom is there, Henry too; Jacintha remains at home with Dina and they will join them later.

It is a grim winter's day; the family vault has been opened and Julia will join her father and mother, brother and sisters. The gravediggers stand mute, respectful and petrified with cold in thin and ragged clothes; Thornton reads poems by Julia's father then one by Keats and another by Shelley. Silence falls and Jane leans against Tom, who holds her tight. The earth scatters on the simple coffin.

JULIA'S SHILLING

Jane is tall for a woman, she and Julia used to joke about it as Julia was a good five inches shorter. They had agreed she would drop Janey when she started singing professionally so she sings as Jane Williams. She is dressed simply but well; her black barathea coat has always been hers; it shows no sign of alterations or turning; her broad brimmed hat frames her well cut features and her hair is as blonde and curly as it was when she was a child. Her face shows the strain of the last few weeks, when Julia's tuberculosis finally claimed her; little to do but keep her comfortable and wait for the end, no relief except laudanum. Every day she slept more; her chest rattled and heaved and she took little sustenance; everything about her shrank except for her eyes, bright in her thin face. 'If I were a dog you would shoot me!' she had said more than once. Mrs Hornton sits with her in the day, for Julia never moved from her first rooms and Mrs Hornton and she were good friends; the old lady's distress was great. 'Who would have thought she would go before me?' For she has come to love her as the daughter she had never had. Jane came most evenings and sat until late, when a cab came for her. Edward had visited regularly until a few months ago, when he gave up all hope and married an eighteen year old, bearing her off to Essex and the life he had so craved for Julia.

The family returns to Jacintha's house where numerous relatives are assembled, young and old, like the Phalanstery but with a generation gone. Dina is weeping and says over and over again, 'She was too young!' and glares at Trelawny as if she begrudges him his life in the absence of Julia. How can he still be here, eighty years old, no stick, compos mentis, and although she cannot know it, to be around until he's eighty-eight. Claire cannot be here: she has written from Florence, where she lives in the via Romana with Paulina, preyed upon by literary thieves who are convinced she holds Shelley's papers. But Claire is a match for them and becomes the inspiration for a famous novel[2], an appropriate legacy.

Tom is telling Jane the latest news of his growing family; four children, his wife a cousin of the Johnsons; he was disappointed that Edward had finally married and brought a newcomer into the family. But he would continue to manage the farm for Edward, who now spends his time painting.

'But what did you expect?' says Jane. 'Julia was never going to marry. She loved her music and you and me and her independence. Even when money became tight during her illness she was resolute. She lived off the annuity and Mrs Horton conveniently forgot the rent, rather than lose her!'

Jacintha hears a knock at the door and comes back into the room bringing with her a tall, bearded young man, carrying a bright faced toddler. Jane's face lights up and she reaches for the little girl, kissing both her and her father. Trelawny heaves towards them.

'Another Julia?' he breathes, craggy face close to the child.

'Yes, indeed,' says Jane firmly, 'but not a Trelawny. Julia was adamant about that.' She feels she is being cruel, but it is true; Julia loved the idea of Jane's child being named after her, but had drawn the line at continuing her second name.

---

[2] *The Aspern Papers* by Henry James.

The old man withdraws to a kindlier conversation with Thornton, whom he still thinks of as a little boy in Italy. Arthur, bending to whisper in Jane's ear, says, 'It's time to go, dearest. I've kept the cab outside; we need to be at Stratton Street for the recital this evening.' She nods; their life is busy: Arthur, the youngest professor at the Academy, and Jane, greatly sought after for private recitals and public concerts. She has even tested the Albert Hall acoustics for the Queen. Their income is good, with Arthur's small private income, and Jane's respectability assured as she works with her husband. They intend to have a sibling or two for little Julia, but both agreed that more would compromise their music. Julia had been delighted and amused. 'Progress at last!' she had said.

Out into the dreary afternoon they go, after a round of farewells, the most difficult with Tom. Despite the trains, Essex was far from London with the demands of the farm and his family, and Jane's and Arthur's lives are not only performances but rehearsals, **practise** and lecturing. The most time they all get together is a week on the farm in the summer, which is wonderful when it happens. Thin rain has started to fall and Arthur wraps his cloak around the contented child and helps his wife into the cab. This journey has been a frequent one during Julia's last illness; their terraced house in Kensington has often been her home for several days at a time to give Mrs Hornton a rest. The horse trots lightly, sensing that this might be the home stretch, and that he might well have quite a few hours rest before the morning; suddenly the cabbie reins him in and shouts that he wants to water the horse now as the water is plentiful in the public trough, better than at his mews. The cab clatters to a halt. Jane looks out.

'Let her watch the horse drinking,' she says to Arthur. He climbs down, carrying the child, and after a moment, Jane follows him. They stand together in the dim street as the horse drinks thirstily and the cabbie whistles softly to him. Jane guides little Julia's hand to stroke the silky nose, then suddenly stops. Her eyes shine in the gloom.

'This is it!' she whispers. 'This is where Tom brought me to meet Julia all those years ago, by those steps! I was so frightened I could barely look at her! Oh darling,' and she clasps her little girl tightly to her, 'how lucky I was to meet such generosity!'

Arthur smiles and takes the child from her. He has heard this story but they have never thought to find the place; he knows all the details down to the shilling that had originally been offered to Tom. They get back into the cab and outside their house he watches as his wife helps the child clamber up the steps to their front door. He pays the driver then adds an extra shilling.

'Spend it well. A shilling can turn a life around.' And he watches as the man tips his hat in grateful surprise and disappears into the gathering night.

A FINAL NOTE

All the imagination needs is the stimulus of facts, said Barry Unsworth, exemplary historical novelist, so, thanks to him and all the census gatherers who have worked since 1841 to compile records of where people lived, so that Julia and her family can be followed round London and Essex: all the registrars who write so clearly the death and birth certificates of all our families: all the biographers whose work must end with facts, but whose facts provide the roots of a good story.

And to:

Julia Trelawny Hunt: 1826-1872

Leigh Hunt: 1784-1859

Charles Dickens: 1812-1870

Catherine Dickens: 1815-1879

Angela Burdett Coutts: 1814-1906

Henry Sylvan Hunt: 1819-1876

Thornton Hunt: 1810-1873

Marianne Hunt: 1788-1857

Rosalind Hunt: 1821-1880

Jacintha Cheltnam née Hunt: 1828-1914

Edward John Trelawny: 1792-1881

Edward Johnson: 1825-1896

Claire Clairmont: 1798-1879

Gordon George, Lord Byron: 1788-1824

Percy Bysshe Shelley: 1792-1822

Fanny Johnson: 1814-1906

And to Tom and Janey Carter; Carlo, Conte D'Orsini; Maria and Alberto who do not appear in any records or censuses.

To Mrs Hornton who appears as Mrs Griffiths on Julia's death certificate.

And to Joan Ward, Chris Walsh, Susan Kelly, Annabel Shirt, Béatrice Laurent Hewitt, Karen Faustini and Yuko Mochizuki Moffett.

Made in the USA
Lexington, KY
07 October 2018